Whateve...
Could Ta...
Tayl...

Now that he knew they... wanted her.

Tonight. Badly.

He shook his head and muttered under his breath. One kiss and he wanted it all. And it wasn't simply physical; that was the problem. He cared too much for this woman.

He'd seen it coming and he'd done nothing to stop it. He'd seen the look in her eyes and known she was beginning to care too much… The evidence was in the generous and giving heart of Taylor that he had seen every time he'd looked deep into her eyes.

He growled in frustration. He couldn't saddle her with this. No matter how willing she might be to accept him as he was. She deserved more. Much more. And until he could give it to her, he had to bring to a halt feelings that were getting far too out of hand.

It had been nearly impossible to ask her to leave tonight. And he doubted if he could ever muster the courage to do it again…

Dear Reader

It's February, the month to celebrate love—which is what Silhouette Desire does every month of the year, of course! Still, we have an extra special line-up of sensual, emotional stories for you this month—so enjoy…

You don't get much more sensual than Diana Palmer's writing. She's back this month with *Champagne Girl* where brooding Matt Kincaid gives young Catherine Blake her first taste of passion. And in the month of romantic gestures, Anne McAllister's Cash Callahan goes for the ultimate! He bursts into the church to stop the woman he loves from marrying another man.

Millionaire Luke Walker is trying to cut passion *out* of his life in *Bride Candidate No. 9*—don't worry, he soon changes his mind! And another misguided bachelor sees the error of his ways this month, in the latest novel from Lass Small.

Finally, Barbara McCauley brings us a *Courtship in Granite Ridge* and don't miss the moving conclusion to the **Montana Malones** trilogy from Anne Eames.

Happy Valentine's Day!

The Editors

Last of the Joeville Lovers

ANNE EAMES

™ SILHOUETTE
Desire ®

Silhouette, Silhouette Desire and Colophon
are registered trademarks of Harlequin Books S.A.,
used under licence.

First published in Great Britain 1999
Silhouette Books, Eton House, 18-24 Paradise Road,
Richmond, Surrey TW9 1SR

© Creative Business Services, Inc. 1998

ISBN 0 373 76142 2

22-9902

Printed and bound in Spain
by Litografia Rosés S.A., Barcelona

ANNE EAMES

This is Anne's sixth novel for Desire™. Her books have appeared on the *USA Today* bestseller list. Anne and her husband, Bill, live in Michigan, U.S.A.

Other novels by Anne Eames

Silhouette Desire®

With special thanks to my pilot buddy, Barry;
to Dana and Christopher Reeve for their inspiration;
and most important, to my favourite cowboy
and love of my life, Bill.

One

"**D**on't you dare stop now!" From her position on the floor, Taylor Phillips stared down into the tired cowboy's eyes and saw beads of sweat streaking down his temples.

"How much longer till you're satisfied?" Josh asked, pumping yet another time.

"At least a minute...five if you can hold out that long."

He groaned and kept moving, but without much enthusiasm.

"Having problems, Joshua Malone? I thought you told me you were in good shape." She knew she was goading him. She also knew that if she could elicit a little anger, he might find more energy and push his own limit.

Finally, with one last growl, he slumped on the floor beneath her. "Enough." A dumbbell rolled free from his hand and coasted along the mat.

Taylor's smile was one of triumph. She checked her watch then stood and extended an arm to Josh. "Not bad.

Four minutes longer than yesterday." Using his good arm, he grabbed hold of her hand and hoisted himself up.

"Where did you learn to be a physical therapist? The University of S and M?" He wiped his forehead on the sleeve of his T-shirt, then massaged his left shoulder.

Taylor laughed at his barb and made notes in his chart, resisting the temptation to write her thoughts: rich kid has to work hard. Poor baby. Out of the corner of her eye she could see him staring at her with that sexy smirk of his, one that he'd probably practiced in front of the mirror and that she'd heard worked on many an unsuspecting female in Bozeman. She wondered if he had a clue how much she enjoyed ignoring his overt moves on her. His shoulder had healed weeks ago. She knew why he kept coming around.

With her head still down she was finishing her notes when the sound of Max's footsteps crossing the tile floor forced her to look up. His face was grave, a cordless phone pressed to his chest.

Josh ignored the ominous body language and tried to engage his father in playful banter. "Hey, Dad...did you teach Taylor to be this tough?"

His expression unchanged, Max didn't acknowledge his son's question. "Josh...you'll have to excuse us a moment. There's an urgent call from Ann Arbor." Max turned back to Taylor. "It's your father," he said and handed her the phone.

Taylor stared at it, her pulse quickening. Her father would never call her at the Malone ranch when he knew she would be working in Max's clinic...especially at this hour of the morning...unless....

She punched a button and spoke into the receiver, trying to steel herself for bad news. "Dad?" The sound of his voice at once confirmed her fears. Something was gravely wrong.

And it had to do with her mother.

Taylor walked around the corner to the office where Max's daughter-in-law, Savannah, sat cross-legged on the floor. Her young son, Billy, knelt beside her, watching as she changed his baby brother's diapers. Savannah's quick smile faded as soon as she saw Taylor's face.

Taylor dropped into a chair in front of the desk and listened intently to her father. "Who's her doctor?" she finally asked. When her father answered, she stood and paced to the window behind the desk. "I'll catch the next flight out. Tell her to hang on, Dad. I'm on my way." Her knees started to shake and she was thankful when he said goodbye.

She switched off the phone and stared at miles of wildflowers leading to the MoJoe Mountains and the mirrored blue waters below, her thoughts turning inward. She had always known this day might come. And she had always known what she would do if it did.

"Taylor?"

She turned and saw the concern on Savannah's face.

"What can I do to help?" she asked, as Max and Josh walked through the doorway.

Max stepped forward. "Let me call the airlines and get you a ticket."

Taylor nodded, still stunned by the news. "I'll have to go home and pack a few things. I don't know how long I'll be gone—"

Max closed the space between them, the pain on his face evident, reminding her that her mother and Max had been friends years ago, that she wasn't some anonymous critical patient. "We'll manage here. Put it out of your mind." He bracketed her shoulders with a gentle touch. "But I don't think you should drive."

She started to protest when Josh broke in. "I'll take you to the airport."

Savannah adjusted her restless six-month-old on one hip and frowned at her watch. "If I remember correctly, the last time I thought about going back to Detroit, the only flight left before noon. If that's still true, there won't be time for you to go home first. I'm not sure if you can even make the flight.''

One way or the other, she would be on that plane. Clothes or no clothes. She tried to remember what still might be hanging in her childhood Ann Arbor home. Then Savannah offered a better solution.

''Between Jenny and me we have plenty of things you could borrow. Why don't we go work on that while Max checks on the flight.''

Taylor let herself be led out of the office and down the hall to the living quarters, feeling as though she were a sleepwalker in a bad dream. In no time at all, Savannah deposited baby Chris in his playpen, told Billy to keep his little brother company, and then proceeded to pull two bags from the closet.

''I have an extra blow-dryer and curling iron. I'll pack them and some personal stuff in this carry-on…but I think Jenny's clothes might be closer to your size.'' She handed a hang-up bag to Taylor and turned her toward the door.

''Thank you,'' she mumbled and picked up her pace to the kitchen where she knew she would find Jenny preparing lunch. With any luck, possibly Ryder or Shane might be there, too. Savannah's or Jenny's husband would make a better traveling companion than Josh. She'd managed to ignore the youngest brother for the few months she'd worked here, except recently when he dislocated his shoulder. Therapy was one thing; spending a couple of hours in a car with him was quite another.

She could always drive herself, she thought as she heard laughter coming from the kitchen. She held out her hands and noticed her trembling fingers and knew that wouldn't be wise. Finally she let out a pent-up breath and pushed through the swinging door to the lively kitchen. If she had to go with Josh, so be it. Reaching her mother on time was all that mattered.

Hannah, the barrel-shaped housekeeper, and Jenny were laughing at something and they turned in unison when she entered the room, their smiles disappearing when they saw her.

"My mom is very sick and I have to leave for the airport." She heard the quaver in her voice and bit her bottom lip. She blinked hard, fighting to clear her vision, and eyed Jenny. "Savannah thought you might lend me some clothes—"

Jenny padded from behind the counter, wiping her hands on the apron that stretched across her rounded belly. "Of course." She hooked Taylor's arm and headed for the side door. "Come on to the cabin with me. Pick out whatever you want. I won't be needing any of it for months."

They started across the gravel drive and cut through the stables, Jenny moving briskly for a woman six months pregnant expecting twins. Since Taylor had accepted this part-time job, she and Jenny hadn't exactly been bosom buddies, but they weren't adversaries, either. Taylor suspected her shunning of Joshua had something to do with Jenny's coolness. But whatever the strain between them, Jenny showed none of it now as she rushed Taylor along.

Neither Ryder or Shane was anywhere in sight, and the horses were all outside in the corral. Sunlight streamed through the open doors, and the smell of fresh-strewn hay rose up to meet her. Outside again, they crossed to the cabin steps and Taylor followed Jenny past the screen door and into the cozy living room beyond, too numb to take in the unfamiliar surroundings. Together they filled the hang-up bag with a couple of simple summer dresses, skirts, knitted tops and jeans.

"Thanks," Taylor said, zipping closed the bag, eager to be on the road.

When they returned to the main house, Max was staring out the back window of the kitchen and Josh was on the phone. He hung up and said, "There! Got everything covered for the rest of the day." He faced Taylor and rubbed his hands together. "Ready to go?"

Taylor hid her disappointment the best she could. Even

if Josh wasn't her first choice, he was doing her a favor.
"Yes, I think so."

Savannah held up a pair of shoes in either hand.
"Thought you could use these…if they fit."

Taylor checked the size and nodded, then glanced over
at the sad figure in front of the window. Max seemed as
dazed as she felt. Savannah found a pocket for the shoes
and zipped the bag closed, the sound snapping Max from
his reverie.

He walked quickly to Taylor's side, acting as though he
only now realized she had returned. "I got you a seat…out
of Bozeman…but you'll have to hurry." He lifted his wrist
and read the time. "The plane leaves in less than two
hours."

Josh gave him a dismissive wave. "Not to worry, Dad.
I'll use my plane and get her there with time to spare."

Max gave him a stern look. "I thought you said it needed
repair."

Josh shrugged. "Nah, just a few minor adjustments. I
took care of it yesterday."

Taylor grimaced. Just what she needed—to squeeze into
some small crop duster and put her life in the hands of this
gamesome cowboy.

Max's expression looked as if he mirrored her thoughts
as he touched Taylor's arm, but then he changed the subject. "Tell your mom I—" he paused and glanced at the
other worried faces in the kitchen "—tell her we'll all be
praying for her."

Taylor held his gaze a moment, certain he wanted to say
more, but he didn't. The women gave her a quick hug, and
Josh tugged at her elbow. He winked and ushered Taylor
outside, where his dusty red pickup was parked at a reckless
angle. She settled quickly into the passenger seat and
strapped herself in as Josh tossed her bags in the back and
slid behind the wheel. He turned the key in the ignition and
looked over at her.

"Don't look so worried. I'm fast, but I'm safe."

She bit her tongue and rolled her eyes. She wanted to say she'd heard that about him from too many coeds, and also at the hospital where she and Max worked when they weren't at the clinic, but she decided now wasn't the time.

Without waiting for a response, he threw the gearshift into reverse, spun into a half circle and sent gravel spitting in all directions as he barreled down the drive to the main gate and cut sharply onto the road heading north toward his hangar. Taylor gritted her teeth and clung to the armrest, telling herself speed was imperative, and that the roads were dry and safe.

Whatever anxiety she'd felt escalated when they stepped into Josh's small Cessna and then taxied to the short grassy runway. She wanted to ask him how long he'd been doing this, but decided it was too late and she really didn't want to know.

The takeoff was smooth and uneventful, and she started to relax. If her mind wasn't elsewhere, she would have enjoyed the mountains on the horizon and the patchwork fields of vivid color below. It was a beautiful day in May by anyone's standards. The sun shone bright in the awesome big skies she'd come to love. On a wistful sigh she remembered that when she was a little girl in Ann Arbor this was just the kind of day her mother had described. It was Mom's stories of her own youth, growing up in Montana and getting her nursing degree from Montana State, that had compelled Taylor to enroll at her mother's alma mater and see for herself the grandeur of this magnificent part of the country.

Taylor leaned her head back and closed her eyes. Mom had been right. It was gorgeous out here. But at times like this, she wished Michigan wasn't so far away.

Please, God, give Mama the strength to hold on.

She felt a tear trickle down her cheek, and she dug for a tissue in her purse, wiping her face quickly and blowing her nose.

"I hope everything works out okay," Josh said.

She wadded the tissue and shoved it into her jeans pocket, realizing for the first time that she still wore her white jacket from the clinic. "Me, too," she said, and shrugged out of it.

"Would you like some music? I have tapes and head-phones." He half shouted over the steady roar of the engine.

She eyed him curiously, surprised at his suddenly somber demeanor. "No, but thank you," she said after a moment. He looked distracted by private thoughts and she wondered where he was.

"Has your mom been sick for a while?" Josh glanced over, then back to the vast blue sky.

She wished he would stop talking. She wasn't in the mood for idle chatter. Still, she was indebted to him for his help, so she answered him with as few words as possible. "Mom was in an auto accident when I was in nursery school. Got pretty banged up. Broke one arm and leg...and lost a kidney. She was in the hospital a long time and then physical therapy after that."

"Is that how you became interested in PT?"

"Yeah, I guess it was." She exhaled loudly, deciding to mollify him and hoping a little conversation might pass time. She felt a slow smile curve her lips as she thought more about his question. "I remember playing nurse with my dolls. I was so proud of Mom and loved to see her in those white uniforms. But after helping her with her exercises when she got home...well, I saw how much it made a difference. She recovered completely and was able to return to work. I thought—" she felt the lump at the back of her throat again "—I hoped it would never come to this, though."

"This?"

"She's in renal failure...the other kidney—" She turned back to the side window and swallowed hard.

"Is she a candidate for a transplant?"

"She's on the list, but the timing..." Taylor heaved a

sigh and decided to tell Josh what was really on her mind. Maybe saying it out loud would give her more confidence. "If there isn't a donor by the time I get there, I'm giving Mom one of mine."

She glanced at him, half expecting him to argue the dangers. His jaw muscles knotted and he didn't comment for the longest time. Then he said, "I wish I could've done something to help my mother."

Taylor stared at him, waiting for more, but nothing came. It was common knowledge at the hospital that Max was widowed, yet she'd never been sure what had happened. How could Josh have helped her? There had been gossip about a possible suicide, but no one seemed certain. It had occurred years before her arrival on campus, and Dr. Max Malone wasn't one to provide grist for the rumor mill. His private life was just that.

Whether in the classroom or seeing to patients at the hospital or his home clinic, Max was all business. He had a tender and caring heart, but beyond that, he was pretty tight-lipped. If Mom hadn't told her stories of the techniques he'd pioneered in orthopedic surgery at the University of Michigan Hospital, Taylor might never have known what a remarkable doctor he was. She'd been truly lucky to have such a man as her mentor.

Suddenly Josh pasted on a toothy smile and looked her way, putting aside whatever had been churning behind his troubled blue-gray eyes. "You're a brave woman, Taylor Phillips."

She chuckled softly. "I don't know about that. I try not to think of the surgery and afterward. I just know I have to do something." He winked at her in that roguish way of his and returned his attention to the skies ahead, falling silent once again.

Why did he play these constant games? For a while she'd thought she'd seen a glimpse of the real man, but the curtain had closed. Once again he took on the air of a carefree playboy and she felt a wave of disappointment, not certain why. Curious, she studied his sun-streaked sandy hair, which hung carelessly over the collar of his aviator jacket, and she wondered if he worked at this unruly look or if it came naturally with his behavior.

He banked the plane unexpectedly, and she jerked against her seat belt. Annoyed she turned her head and muttered caustically under her breath. "Fast with cars, planes and women. What a man!"

"Excuse me?"

"Nothing. I—" The single engine sputtered and the nose dipped radically. She gripped her armrests. "What was that?"

He leveled the plane, seeming unconcerned. "She's an old plane. Don't worry about it. Everything's okay."

She spotted the airport just ahead and wished they were on the ground safely.

"Next time I take you for a ride, I'll have my new plane and you won't look so worried."

She crossed her arms and tried to relax, glad the engine noise had returned to normal and that they had begun their descent.

A new plane, she thought. Must be nice. Here she would be paying on student loans well into the twenty-first century, and this guy's talking about buying a plane as if it were no bigger deal than a pair of boots. She'd been right to think he was a self-centered, spoiled—

"Will you call and let us know how your mom is doing?"

Taylor stared at him a moment. Who was this man? And why was she even wasting time trying to figure him out?

Josh glanced over when she didn't answer.

"Y-yes. Sure." She closed her mouth and watched the smooth landing, shrugging all thoughts of Joshua Malone from her head and worrying once again about the days ahead.

She would make her plane without a problem. If only there wasn't a layover in Minneapolis—it would take at least another seven hours until she reached her mother's side.

Please, God. Don't let me be too late.

Josh helped her down the steps and carried her bags across the tarmac to the terminal. Taylor seemed a million miles away and he understood. He wished he could think of appropriate words to comfort her, but he remembered hearing all the platitudes after his mother's death and how he'd felt. So he remained silent and walked alongside her to the gate.

He stayed with Taylor until her row was called, then he wished her good luck and watched her move gracefully down the jetway.

A feeling of anxiety stirred behind his rib cage. He didn't know why or when the game had changed, but he knew it had. Taylor Phillips was no longer just another challenge. He was starting to care about this woman—what made her tick, what would happen to her in Ann Arbor, and when would she return?

He spun on his heel and strode toward the exit.

How had he let this happen?

Two

The men's room door opened ahead of Taylor as she neared the entrance to Intensive Care, and the sad figure of John Phillips emerged. At first he didn't notice her, his head down, shoulders rounded, no doubt from fatigue as well as worry.

"Dad!" She moved quickly to him and welcomed his warm embrace. He squeezed her tight, and for the longest time said nothing. Over her father's shoulder she said gently, "It's going to be okay, Dad. I've made a decision."

He stepped back and eyed her curiously, his face looking more lined than she'd ever remembered. Taylor took him by the shoulders and stared into his weary dark eyes, hoping to instill a measure of hope in him. "I'm going to give Mom one of my kidneys." He started to shake his head, but she stilled it between her hands. "There's no point arguing with me. While I'm seeing Mom, would you try finding her doctor…have him paged, if need be." She looked around them and added, "Where's Michael?"

"Your brother's in the chapel." He stared at the tile floor. "Sweetheart—"

"Please, Dad. Just find the doctor. Let's not waste time." She kissed his cheek as if he'd agreed and then punched the metal square on the wall. The large double doors to ICU swung open and she raced to the desk beyond.

"I'm here to see Angela Phillips. I'm her daughter."

"Room six to the right…but you can only stay a few minutes."

"Thank you." She tore around the corner, found the room and came to an abrupt stop in the doorway. Tubes ran to bags and monitors in all directions. She'd seen it hundreds of times before, but none had been her mother…except for that one time years ago after the car wreck. Then, like now, Mom seemed so frail and vulnerable, so unlike the vibrant and energetic woman she had always been.

Angela's eyelids fluttered, then opened to narrow slits when she rolled her head toward the door. Taylor let out a cleansing breath and raced to her mother's side.

"Taylor—" Angela reached out a shaky hand, IVs channeled through a heplock into a puffy vein. "I'm so glad you made it—"

In time. Those were the words that hung between them, but Taylor refused to believe them.

"Mom, you have to fight this." Then she forced a smile. "You're getting a new kidney. Everything's going to be all right."

Angela closed her eyes and a sweet smile curved her lips. "I can't let you do that, dear."

"Who said it was me?"

Angela squinted at her with a knowing look.

"Well, I'm going to do it, so there's no point discussing it." Taylor glanced at the monitors and read the numbers. They would have to improve before surgery, but now that Mom knew there was hope, surely she would fight harder.

She had to.

Taylor couldn't imagine life without her mother. They had always been so close, even when separated by miles. The weekly Sunday night phone calls were followed by long, chatty letters. There was nothing they didn't share.

"Taylor?" Angela whispered, as she closed her eyes again.

Taylor leaned across the railing and kissed her mother's clammy forehead. "I'm right here, Mama." She kept her face near, and Angela's lips barely moved.

"You have to do something for me—"

"Anything, Mama." She swallowed hard to keep from crying. She had never seen her mother this sick, not even after the accident.

Angela squeezed Taylor's hand and she watched tears escape from behind her mother's closed lids. "Please don't hate me—"

"Don't talk silly," she said, interrupting what she guessed were delirious words. "I could never hate you, Mama. You know how much I love you."

Angela nodded her head ever so slightly. "There's something in the attic that you have to find for me...but you can't let your father see...."

Taylor looked nervously behind her, relieved that her father had not yet returned. What on earth was her mother talking about? Was it the drugs?

"Under the old love seat in the attic...loose boards...two journals I wrote...long ago." Her words were coming in short bursts and Taylor thought of making her stop. "Don't let anyone see them." She opened her eyes slowly and held her daughter's steady gaze. "Please?"

What on earth could this mean? Her parents never kept secrets from each other. She was sure of it. They had always treated each other with such tenderness and respect; there was always such contentment between them. It had to be the drugs.

"Taylor? Will you get them for me?"

Hallucinating or not, she couldn't say no. "Yes, Mama."

She kissed her mother's cheek and smoothed her fair hair away from her sallow face. "Get some rest now, okay? I'll be back later."

Angela closed her eyes and seemed instantly asleep. Taylor checked the monitors again and there was no change. She pressed her lips to her mother's temple and whispered in her ear, "Fight hard, Mama. I love you," thinking she probably didn't hear.

Her eyes still closed, Angela whispered back, "I love you, too."

With one last lingering look, Taylor backed quietly out of the room.

Michael and Dad were leaning against the far wall, arms folded as if to ward off a sudden chill. Michael met her halfway for a frightened hug as her father pulled himself from a stupor.

His head shot up and his eyes grew round. "Is she—?"

"She's resting."

He exhaled a loud breath and Taylor realized what he'd been thinking.

"Did you find her doctor?"

He nodded, then clasped her hand between both of his. "I told him what you said." He averted his eyes and she could see them glazing over. "He said she's too sick for a transplant." He looked back. "I'm so sorry, sweetheart. It's just too late."

"No!" Taylor backed away and glared at him. "Mom's a fighter. She'll get better and we'll do the surgery." She lowered her voice and raised his chin with her finger, forcing him to meet her gaze. "Dad...you can't give up or Mom will see it on your face."

"You're right," he said, but without much conviction. "Let me go in and kiss her good-night. The doctor suggested we go home and let her rest. They'll call if there's any change." He stumbled toward the door, paused, straightened his shoulders some and walked toward the woman who had been his wife and best friend for nearly thirty years.

Michael laced Taylor's fingers in his. "Where are your bags?"

She stared after their father, unable to look Michael in the eye. Maybe she could fool Dad with her false hopes, but Michael could always see right through her. He was only twenty, five years her junior, yet it had been years since she'd thought of him as a kid. She met his sad gray eyes and remembered his question. "My bags are downstairs behind the information counter, but—"

"I know you want to stay, but if you don't leave, neither will Dad. I'm worried about him. I can't remember when he slept last."

She didn't want to leave, but she knew Michael was right. And then there was the matter of her mother's request. Was there really something in the attic beneath loose boards? If there was and she could tell Mom she had found it and removed it, maybe it would buoy her spirits. It was grabbing at straws, but that was all she had at the moment.

Her father joined them in the hall, his chin back on his chest.

Taylor took his arm, and Michael moved to the opposite side. "Let's go home, Dad. She'll be better in the morning." Her words sounded hollow to her own ears, yet like a gentle breeze, they fanned a low flame of hope.

After a fitful night of half expecting the phone to ring, at dawn Taylor sat up with a start when she heard her father tell Michael that he was taking a shower and to listen for the phone.

All night she had thought about her mother's request and wished she could go exploring upstairs. But the night had been too still and the house too small for her to hide her movements, so she had waited. Now, as soon as she heard the water running, Taylor checked that Michael's door was closed before darting up the attic stairs.

It had been years since she'd ventured up here, and the dusty smell of cardboard boxes and stored treasures reminded her of lazy afternoons with Mom, times when they had retraced the steps of old shoes and hats left behind by Grandma and Aunt Helen. Taylor stopped at the top step and eyed the old rocker in front of the window. A floor lamp with an arched neck and Tiffany shade waited next to the rocker for someone to pull its chain. Cross-stitched throw pillows rested at the foot of it all, where Taylor used to sit by the hour and listen to her mother's stories of the Big Sky Country of her youth.

Particles of sunshine filtered through the aged organza curtains and spotlighted the old love seat on the opposite wall. The curved cherry wood trim on the back was in better shape than the willow green brocade upholstery. She could almost hear the cushions ripping if she dared sit on its fragile surface. She walked cautiously toward it, having no intention of sitting on it at all, wishing she didn't have to touch it. If there *were* loose boards beneath it, she hoped they revealed nothing. Yet the sound of her own fast breathing told her there would be something there. Something she wasn't sure she wanted to discover. Something that might tip the scales of their balanced little family, a good and loving family that was at the core of who she was.

Taylor stopped at one end of the small sofa, her arms still at her side. She closed her eyes and pictured her mother's worried face when she'd made this strange request. There was no going back to the hospital without telling Mom all was safe.

Before she could lose her nerve, she lifted an armrest and moved the sofa silently away from the wall. Wide cracks bracketed two boards beneath and she fought the urge to run from this once-cozy space. Instead, she stooped and tugged at the planks, listening for the water to shut off downstairs, hearing nothing but the hammering of her own heart in her ears.

There, below the floor, were two cloth-covered journals, their delicate calico prints suggesting a woman's loving touch. Taylor retrieved them quickly, replaced the boards and repositioned the love seat in the clean spots left by the claw-footed legs.

With the books tucked safely under her bulky sweater, she descended the stairs, raced to her old room, and pressed her back to the closed door before releasing the breath she'd been holding.

There. She had Mama's journals. Dad would never see them, would never know their content.

But what did they say that would hurt him so much?

There was a soft rap on the door and Taylor jumped.

"Taylor?"

Quickly she hid the books in her carry-on bag and then took a cleansing breath.

"Be right there, Dad." Suddenly she felt as though she were part of some conspiracy. Would he see a guilty look on her face? She glanced at the mirror and practiced a calm she didn't feel, then opened the door.

"Are you okay, sweetheart?"

His concern doubled her guilt and she struggled to conceal it. She'd had no reason to ever deceive her father before, but Mom had said he must never know. "I—I'm fine, Dad. Maybe we should leave for the hospital now."

His weary gaze lingered on her face a moment and her pulse raced. But then he turned and headed for the door, Michael right behind him. "Yes. I think we should get going."

When they arrived at the room, they were blocked by a wall of white and aqua jackets surrounding Angela's bed. Orders were barked and obeyed. Taylor stood on one foot then the other trying to see the monitors, but the view was obstructed by a burly intern whose pinched brow and intense eyes gave her reason to worry. She squeezed Michael's sweaty palm and felt her father's hand dig deeper into her shoulder.

It was at times like this that Taylor wished she knew less about medicine, that she was a little girl again...who thought her mother was invincible.

Her ear was trained on the beeps from the monitor, picturing each peak, praying for the next. And then she heard the sound she feared the most—a constant hum.

Injections and paddles followed the dismal sound, but to no avail.

The time of death was called by the senior physician.

The trio huddled in the doorway, Taylor in the center. She closed her eyes and pictured her mother's soul winging its way to heaven and tried to draw comfort from the fact that she was in a better place now, free of all pain. It helped a little, and surely as time passed her faith would help her again.

But in the deep recesses of her mind, there was a dark dread that in the months to come Mom's death would only be part of her grieving. Grandmother used to say trouble came in threes. If she was right, Taylor didn't speculate on number two and three. At the moment one seemed more than enough.

It came as no surprise to any of them when the family read Angela's letters Wednesday afternoon. There was one for each of them that they would later share, and there was one that listed the whereabouts of valuables and papers of importance. Angela had anticipated this day and had planned every last detail, including prepayment of expenses. She'd asked to be cremated after a private family viewing, and if they decided to have a memorial service, she hoped it would be the next day at the hospital chapel.

Simple, clean, fast.

That's what she wanted and that's what she got, the family somewhat relieved that decisions had been made, all too numb with the loss of a young, vital woman.

Phone calls kept them busy until late evening, when her father and Michael each retreated behind closed doors, leaving Taylor alone in the kitchen. She cleaned up the bowls of half-eaten soup and wiped the counter, noticing her mother's hair appointment marked on the calendar next to the phone. It was for next Thursday.

Later, she told herself. She'd call the shop tomorrow.

The idea of telling the sad story one more time today left her weak in the knees and she slumped into the nearest chair. She'd held it together all day, as much for her father and Michael's sake as her own. Right now she could use a good cry, alone in her room.

But there was one more call she had to make.

Not only had she promised Josh she'd call, but she knew Max would want to know. Josh. She remembered their conversation on the plane and his faraway look when he'd spoken of his mother. The pain had shown on his face, even after all these years. The knot at the back of her throat pushed again as she forced herself out of the chair and to the phone.

Hannah answered on the second ring and said she was the only one home. Taylor rushed through the bad news, surprised when the tough old housekeeper started sniffling and then blew her nose. They didn't know each other that well; the reaction seemed out of character. And what seemed even stranger were her parting words.

"Call Max after the funeral tomorrow, will ya, sweetie?"

Taylor paused a moment, then said, "Sure."

When she hung up the phone and padded into her room, she wondered why she should call Max again. Maybe to talk about when she would be back to work.

The room down the hall from the hospital chapel was filled to capacity with food and those who had come to pay their respects.

Taylor accepted the sympathetic touches and hugs from hundreds, faces blurring together, kind words washing over her like rain that wasn't wet, not touching her, not penetrating the cloak she wore around her pain. Dad stood to one side of her, his eyes red rimmed, his composure a thin facade. Michael no longer fought the tears. He bit his top lip and nodded acknowledgment to mourners, never saying a word, his light blue collar spotted with dark droplets.

Mercifully the day ended and the grief-stricken family returned to their little bungalow near the hospital. They reminisced about good times and dug out old photo albums, but eventually the men found solace in their rooms while Taylor sipped her lukewarm tea and stared at the phone on the kitchen wall. As much as the Malones had come to mean to her, Montana and the life she had made there seemed part of a distant past, as surreal as the events of the last couple of days.

Still, she had told Hannah she would call. So she did.

Hannah only said hello this time, before shuffling off to get Max, whose voice sounded as strained as her own.

"I'm so sorry about your mother," he said.

She could hear the pain in his voice and knew his words far transcended politeness. He cared about her mother; they had been friends. "I know." She swallowed, hoping to keep the conversation short. "The flowers were beautiful. Thank the rest of the family for me...please?"

Max said nothing, the tension at the other end of the line nearly palpable. It was as if he were wary about speaking his mind, that there was something else he wanted to say and couldn't. She decided it must be about work.

"I talked to Dad and Michael. We agreed it would be best for all of us to get back to work. They started an addition to someone's house last week that needs a roof before it rains, and—"

"Take as much time as you need. I don't want to rush you."

"You're not. I want to...have to keep busy."

Max didn't argue. In fact, he said nothing. "Max? Is there something you're not telling me?"

The pause, followed by a long sigh, told her there was. "Max?"

"You have enough on your plate—"

"Please. What is it?" She knew it wasn't good, yet she had to know.

"It's Josh—"

She sprang out of the chair and paced toward the sink. "What about Josh?"

"I didn't want to trouble you with this, Taylor, but...well, he had an accident with his plane—"

"Is...is he—"

"It looks like he's going to pull through."

She breathed a sigh of relief, but before she could relax he told her the rest.

"He's banged up pretty bad, and—" Max paused, then blurted it out "—Taylor...he's going to need our help. He's paralyzed from the waist down."

Three

As difficult as the flight had been to Detroit, the return was even worse. The hope Taylor had nursed five days ago had been replaced with a large empty hole, one she doubted would ever be filled, a wound so fresh and deep that she couldn't quite comprehend the days and months ahead. Her work, and a lot of help from above, would be her salvation.

And why did this have to happen to Josh? Was this number two of three, as Grandma had warned? If it was, then what else was in store for her? She shook her head and squared her shoulders, dismissing the silly adage as she strode down the hospital corridor, nodding at familiar faces, her gait saying she had no time for idle chatter.

She stepped into the elevator and punched the button for ICU, then punched it again when it didn't respond, as if the second prompt might speed things along. Others wandered in and she stepped aside. One young man held a large stuffed animal, and his face reflected the joy and pride of a new papa. She stared at the floor and wondered when she might feel joy again.

First Mom, now this. Josh's dimpled smile flashed in her mind's eye. So young, so carefree...so handsome. He had everything.

That wasn't true, she reminded herself. He'd lost a mother, too. At least she had hers for twenty-five years, which was almost twenty years longer than Josh could say. And then another thought crossed her mind: why did people wait for a tragedy to think kindly about certain people? Why did they—she—not see the pain in their eyes before and realize that they carried baggage from the past, too? Like Josh...

The elevator stopped and Taylor excused her way to the front, wondering what she would say to Josh when she saw him. She hadn't been very nice to him in the past, based mostly on rumors and supposition...and her own prejudice against young people with easy money.

Today would be different; she would look Josh in the eye and start again. There was a good man inside there somewhere; she was sure of it. After all, he was Max's son. He had to be. And now, more than ever, Josh would need help to see him through.

As she neared ICU she remembered the pastor's recent eulogy. "When you're feeling your lowest, reach out to someone else in need...it's impossible to feel sad when you're making someone else smile."

Taylor held tight to that thought and identified herself at the nurses' station, then pressed the metal plate on the wall for the big double doors to swing open. Why it had to be Josh whom God had chosen to help occupy her days of mourning, she didn't know. But she made a silent vow that she would do her best to bring a smile back on that handsome face of his.

She stepped into the room and suppressed a moan. Both legs were in traction; a trapeze hung over his chest. Monitors and IVs surrounded him, reminding her of her mother's plight just days ago. With an ache in her chest, she stepped into the room. Josh's head was facing the window and she thought he was asleep, but when her shoes squeaked on the tile floor, he looked at her, and amidst a maze of cuts and bruises a big smile washed over his pale lips.

"Hi, gorgeous." His speech was a little slurred, his tongue sounding thick with drugs. Still, he smiled. "This is much better," he said.

She moved slowly to his side, wanting to touch him, yet feeling shy for some odd reason. "What's much better?" she asked, pretending not to notice the extent of his injuries.

"A beautiful nurse! In the movies, there are always young, pretty nurses. I had just about given up."

Still full of it, she thought, then chuckled. "I'm not a nurse. I'm a—"

"Yeah, yeah. A sadistic physical therapist."

His smile was firmly in place, a fact that amazed her. She had only to enter his room to achieve her goal. Without thinking, she returned his easy smile.

"Guess that shoulder business was just a sample of what I'm in for, huh?"

Taylor straightened his covers, needing something to do with her hands and having trouble holding his gaze. "You got that right, cowboy. You ain't seen nothing yet."

"I love it when you talk tough."

"Yeah, well, we'll see how tough you are in the months to come."

"Months?" He shook his head. "Uh-uh. Weeks. Once I get out of this place, you wait and see. I'll be the best success story you've ever told."

She glanced at his elevated legs, hoping he couldn't read her worries about his paralysis, about the severity of the damage that may have been done. When she looked back at his sleepy face, his smile had disappeared.

"You *will* be my therapist, won't you?"

"Yes. Of course. You were one of my favorite patients

to abuse.'' She swallowed hard and decided it was time to leave. ''I wouldn't miss it for the world,'' she said, and turned to go.

Josh reached out and snagged her hand, his fingers shaking. ''I'm glad.'' He held her gaze a few seconds too long, then, as if sensing her discomfort, he waved his free hand in the direction of his legs. ''It's temporary, you know. Traumatic something-or-other. Nothing hard work can't cure.'' He tried to move and winced. ''I'll just have to pretend it's training camp for football. Used to have a pretty grueling schedule, you know. Two-a-days…that's what they called them. With lots of running and weight lifting in between.'' He stopped talking suddenly and studied her face. ''But the coach never looked as good as you.'' He shot her a roguish wink.

Taylor shook her head, seeing the fear and uncertainty behind all his bravado. ''You never quit, do you?''

''Nope,'' he said, eyeing her closely and still holding her hand.

The feel of his lingering touch sent her pulse racing. She wondered if he was still thinking of physical therapy; she sure wasn't. She caught herself quickly and placed his hand on his chest with a gentle pat. She must remember her objectives: to be his physical therapist and part of his healing process as well as her own.

''You need your rest,'' she said. ''I'll be back later.''

''Promise?''

She forced a lazy smile. ''Promise.''

''Today?''

''If you'd like.''

''I'd like.''

Taylor left the unit, rounded the corner and then stopped, pressing her back to the cold concrete wall and breathing deeply through her mouth. She'd always prided herself in being able to control her emotions. Yes, she had cried over her mother's death and she surely would again, but she knew Mom was in a better place now and that Dad and Michael would take care of each other.

But who would take care of her? She longed for a hug and a shoulder to lean on. That must be why Josh's gentle touch had shaken her so.

She pushed off the wall and headed for Max's office.

Vulnerable. It was only natural that she would feel vulnerable for a while. She would be wise to remember that whenever she was with Josh. He needed her help; she needed to keep busy.

That's all there was to it.

Josh stared out the window, wishing he was on the other side, feeling the sunshine on his face. And more importantly—the ground beneath his feet. He tried focusing on a list of calls that had to be made, chores that had to be delegated. His first crop of wheat needed attention.

Yet the farm was a hazy image eclipsed by a beautiful face, one surrounded by waves of hair fairer than his precious wheat, framing eyes bluer than his beloved Montana sky.

He bent an arm behind his head and pictured her fragile smile, and suddenly guilt prickled in his chest. *Damn.* He'd been so glad to see her, he hadn't even mentioned her mother's death. What an insensitive oaf she must think he is. A self-absorbed oaf. Who better than he knew how it felt to lose a mother? Next time…when she returned.…

He closed his eyes and his head grew fuzzy, the drugs numbing more than his pain. His thoughts were again a jumble and it was hard to concentrate. Wheat fields blurred with blond hair, and yellow combines turned into oak caskets. Then, mercifully, images of mothers and deaths were overtaken by the fluids dripping into the back of his hand and everything went blank again.

Max rose to greet Taylor, stepping quickly from behind his cluttered desk. He gave her a gentle embrace and then sat back on the edge of his desk. "How are you holding up?"

Taylor bit her top lip and nodded, not meeting his dark eyes.

"I wish I could have been there. I'm so sorry—"

She held up a hand, stopping him. This was the worst—hearing someone say they were sorry and seeing the sadness in their eyes. Sometimes she wished everyone would pretend nothing had happened, that they would give her a few days, even hours, to mend.

She was being unkind, she thought, and expelled a long breath.

When the silence became uncomfortable she changed topics. "I just came from Josh's room. His spirits seem good."

Max nodded and looked at the floor.

"How bad is it? Can you tell me?"

Max exhaled loudly. "Too soon to say, but we're optimistic."

"Spinal cord?"

"Not severed."

Taylor dropped into the chair behind her, only now realizing how much she had dreaded another answer. Max took the seat next to her, tugged at a leg of his scrubs and crossed an ankle over one knee. "I keep reminding myself how much worse it could have been. If Shane hadn't been on his way over to the farm when the plane went down—"

"You mean he actually saw the crash?" Bile rose in her throat just thinking about it.

Max shook his head. "Hannah and Jenny had done a lot of baking that morning, and Shane volunteered to drive some things over to the farm. Thank God he was in his Explorer and had his cell phone." Max rubbed his temples and Taylor saw the fatigue and worry on his face. "Josh tipped his wings when he spotted Shane on the road below...the way he likes to do whenever he sees one of us…or at least that's what Shane thought he was doing. Then the plane cleared the trees and—'' Max sucked in air and finished ''—we all heard the impact. The ground shook and I knew…''

Taylor reached out a hand and touched his arm. ''We don't have to talk about this now.''

''No. It's okay.'' He patted the back of her hand. ''Shane called 911 and got to the site soon after. But all he could see was fire and smoke. Then he said he thought he was seeing a mirage. Heat waves rose from the ground and he saw Josh's jacket. He drove as close as he could and dragged Josh far enough away before the explosion.''

''And Shane?''

''Just scrapes and bruises when he hit the ground.'' He uncrossed his legs and braced his elbows on his knees. ''And an unwarranted dose of guilt.''

''Guilt?''

''He can't get it out of his head that he might have done the damage to Josh's legs when he dragged him.''

''But, Max, the alternative—''

Max slapped his knees and stood. ''I know. I've told him that. But until Josh walks again, Shane won't listen to reason.''

Taylor pushed out of her chair and faced Max, feeling the effects of the worst week of her life. ''Then we'll just have to make sure Josh walks again, won't we?'' She tried to smile, but the corners of her mouth wouldn't move.

Max smiled for her. ''If anyone can do it, Taylor, it's you…but it will mean a lot of extra hours. I know the timing couldn't be worse—''

''The timing couldn't be better. I need to work right now.''

He held her gaze and looked as if he wanted to say more. There was so much pain on his tanned face, the gray at his temples more pronounced than she remembered.

''I have a patient in postop. Will you be around a while?''

She nodded. "Either in PT or with Josh."

"Good. There's something we need to talk about." He looked guilty suddenly, and she couldn't imagine what was on his mind. "I—I know this is a terrible imposition, but I was hoping you might move out to the ranch when Josh goes home. He'll need a lot of one-on-one time, and I doubt he'd work as well with me." Taylor opened her mouth to speak, but Max stopped her. "Just think about it. No need to decide now."

Taylor stood rooted in place and watched Max amble down the hall toward Recovery.

Move out to the ranch? The thought hadn't crossed her mind. Yet the idea of too much time alone in her small apartment had worried her. The move could help her as well as Josh.

Then why was she experiencing this shortness of breath? What was she afraid of? She knew and liked the family, and there was plenty of room for her in that big sprawling home.

Finally she puffed out her cheeks, burst out a long breath and headed for the Physical Therapy Unit. It was best not to think about the future right now.

Hard work. Lots of it. That's what she needed.

Time would clear the cobwebs.

The patient load was lighter than usual, giving Taylor too much time to think. Each moment there was a break in the schedule, she thought of Josh upstairs, and confusion swirled in her head. Less than a week ago she didn't even like the man. In fact, she'd gone out of her way to avoid him the few days a week she'd worked at the ranch clinic. Now she couldn't get him out of her thoughts.

He was hurt. He needed her help. Staying at the ranch during his therapy made sense. Logic, logic, logic. It wasn't working this time.

The last patient left and she strode toward Josh's room, drawn there with a force she was too weary to analyze.

When she arrived at his bedside, he opened his eyes and smiled his easy smile again.

"You're back."

"I said I would."

"A woman of her word." He patted the edge of his bed and she sat gingerly. "Hear any good jokes lately?"

She laughed, feeling some of the tension ease. "Afraid not."

His expression grew serious. "I'm sorry. I'm being selfish again." He turned off the TV with the remote on his bed railing, then met Taylor's eyes. "I meant to say something before about your mother—"

Taylor averted her gaze, bracing herself for another "I'm sorry about your loss." But Josh surprised her.

"I know how you feel." He took her hand as he had before and the reaction in her limbs was the same. "Anytime you want to talk…maybe reminisce…you know where to find me." His stroke on the back of her hand felt good. Sincere. "I don't have as many memories as you do," he added, "but I'll tell you a few of mine if you'll tell me some of yours…when you're ready."

Taylor's gaze drifted lazily over the length of his battered body and then returned to his drooping eyelids. In spite of all that had happened to him, his concerns were for her. This didn't quite mesh with her earlier impression of this man. Had he always been this sensitive and she'd missed it? Or was it that her guard was down?

Whichever, she was glad when he closed his eyes, glad that he didn't see the moisture brimming in her own.

She tiptoed from the room and stopped at the front desk, where she'd left her two bags from the airport. They were light, and the distance to her apartment was short, so she decided to walk. The cool evening breeze revived her, and she thought that sometime soon she should make arrangements to get her car from the ranch. Yet in her grief even this little detail seemed to overwhelm her.

She entered her quiet second-floor apartment and just

stood in the middle of the warm dusky room, bags still in hand, not knowing what to do next. Time passed, she wasn't sure how much, before she remembered something important. She walked to her bedroom, opened one bag and found what she was looking for. Gently she lifted the two calico-covered journals and pressed them to her chest.

At last the tears spilled freely. She dropped on the bed and let them come. There was no one watching; she no longer needed to be brave. And when the tears had run their course, she opened her nightstand, slipped the books inside and gently closed the drawer, knowing it would be some time before she was ready to face such personal pages. Someday she would read them. Every word. Then she would know her mother's fears.

A chill trailed through her as she crawled into her cold bed and closed her eyes. The old love seat in the Ann Arbor attic, with its loose floorboards beneath, were her last waking thoughts.

John Phillips traipsed up the attic stairs and braced his weight on one arm of the old love seat. A hand-crocheted throw lay folded neatly over the opposite arm. He remembered the hours of contentment on his wife's face as she'd pulled each stitch of it while patiently awaiting the birth of Taylor.

Memories. There were so many good ones.

Yet there were bad times, too—one nightmare that cut so deep he had been certain at the time that the pain would never leave him, but with the help of God their marriage had more than survived. It had found peace and love again.

Weary to the bone, he lifted the end of the love seat and hunkered down to remove the loose planks. His fingers paused over the cracks in the wood, remembering the time years ago when he'd discovered the journals and the days after when he'd decided not to tell Angela.

Finally he would destroy the only remaining evidence of that dreaded time in their lives. He lifted the boards and stared at the empty space below. Stunned, he sat down with a thump. It had been years since he'd looked here. Perhaps Angela had destroyed them long ago. He rubbed his chest as if it would slow the pounding of his heart. Surely the children hadn't found the journals. Had they?

No. It was unthinkable. If they had, they would have said something. He would have seen the questions in their eyes, a change of some sort.

When his pulse slowed, he returned the boards and love seat to their original place, picked up the handmade throw and took it with him down the stairs, clutching the treasure to him and reassuring himself that the secret was safe at long last.

Four

The scrapes and bruises on Josh's face and arms disappeared over the next couple of weeks, and although no feeling had returned to his legs, his smile seemed as optimistic as ever.

Taylor watched him flex his biceps as he pulled himself up to the bar over his chest. He had long ago abandoned hospital garb in favor of his own white T-shirts, which fit snugly over his well-worked torso. Thankfully his shoulder had healed well. The effects of hard work with his upper body was evident. And distracting. Yes, she was glad to see him working out, though she'd seen other patients do the same, and their results hadn't left her weak in the knees.

"So...when do I get out of here?" Josh asked.

She made herself look at his face, which was no small feat. "That's not for me to decide," she said with a forced calm. He pulled himself up and down on the bar some more, showing off his strength. In the past she'd thought hunky bodies meant empty brains. It seemed where Josh

Malone was concerned, she was usually wrong. Her visits at his bedside had proved it time and again.

"Well, I can get myself in and out of a wheelchair without a problem. Don't you think I could do the rest at home just as easily?"

Shane and Jenny sauntered into the room before Taylor could answer, buying her time to compose her racing thoughts. If Josh went home, was she ready to move to the ranch? To work so closely with him day after day?

Shane backhanded Josh's shoulder. "You causing problems again, little bro?"

"Me?" He looked offended, then smiled. "I just want to get out of here and start walking, that's all."

Jenny planted a noisy kiss on his cheek. "You'd better pretty soon." She smoothed her cotton top over her ever-growing belly and locked her fingers below the big bulge. "Does it look like we can wait forever? Remember your promise, Joshua!"

Taylor watched the family interplay from the foot of the bed and thought of Michael and her father. She missed them more than ever and envied the easy camaraderie of the Malones.

Josh cocked his head and frowned at Jenny. "What promise?"

"You know very well what promise…to be our backup plan if these babies decide to come quickly. Who else can fly us here to the hospital?"

Shane tugged his wife closer. "I could try. Couldn't do much worse than Josh."

"Very funny," Josh said, yet his expression didn't register amusement. He seemed distracted by something and Taylor wondered what. Was he afraid to fly again? She sure would be.

Shane punched his shoulder. "Come on. Lighten up. Since when did you take yourself so seriously?"

Josh stared at his legs and Shane looked as though he'd been stabbed in the gut. He shuffled his feet and then continued. "That Cessna dealer called last night. Said your new plane will be ready soon."

Taylor studied Josh's reaction, but she couldn't be sure how he felt about the news, and he didn't comment.

Jenny tugged at Shane's arm. "We're going to be late for my appointment if we don't get going." She bussed Josh's cheek again and stepped back, taking Shane's hand. She hesitated at the foot of the bed, and Taylor met her questioning look. In that brief instant she thought she saw a challenge in Jenny's eyes that seemed to be saying, Will you be there for him when he needs you most? How much do you really care?

"See you later," Jenny said, talking to Josh, but still sizing up Taylor.

Taylor picked up Josh's chart and pretended not to notice.

Though later that night, on the slow walk home, she asked herself the imagined question, How much *did* she really care?

Just before leaving the hospital she'd told Max she would move out to the ranch—temporarily, of course—and he'd seemed glad. Too much time alone at her apartment had left her indulging her grief far more than she thought she would at the ranch, surrounded by others.

With a heavy heart, she entered her building and trudged up the stairs, knowing there was something else on her mind.

It was time to begin reading her mother's journals.

Today was my first day back to work since Taylor was born and what a day of emotion it was! Dropping my precious little toddler off at the sitter's was like ripping my heart from my chest. Those sad blue eyes when I said goodbye filled me with such guilt. I was tempted to scoop her up in my arms and take her home with me, but I didn't, which made me feel so very selfish.

Why can't I be like other women who are happy

being full-time moms? I love my time with Taylor, but I missed nursing and the company of adults who talked in complete sentences.

When I got to the hospital everyone seemed pleased to see me. There was even a ''Welcome Back'' banner hanging in the nurses' lounge. I called the sitter twice to be certain Taylor was doing well and was grateful to hear she was making new friends and adjusting quickly.

I was a little worried about getting back into the routine at the hospital, but it was as though I had never left. Max was busier than I ever remembered him. Students rushed after him from one postop patient to the next, hanging on his every word. It was good to see him again and something of a surprise. When he returned home to Montana the last time, I didn't expect to see him again. I missed him like crazy, but it was for the best that he left when he did. His three sons are still young, the youngest only a few years older than Taylor. How he manages to live with weekend visits, I'll never understand. He occasionally talks of the boys with a faraway look of tenderness on his face, but then it always turns sad and he changes the subject.

Poor Max. I can't imagine days away from my family. Even though today passed quickly—and I must confess I loved being back—ten hours away from Taylor was long enough. And oh, the joy in my heart when she flung her chubby little arms around my neck and said, ''Mommy, Mommy!''

John was rather cool with me over dinner and didn't want to hear about my day. I wish he could understand why I needed to go back. I wish he could trust that I won't let my other job hurt our little girl. In time I hope he'll see I made the right decision.

Taylor closed the journal and returned it to the drawer, then brushed the tears from her cheeks. As much as it hurt to know she would never feel her arms around her mother's neck again, she drew comfort from Mom's words of love and knew she would treasure every page. Theirs had been a special relationship that would remain in her heart forever.

She closed her eyes and let the exhaustion of the day begin to claim her, making one last mental note. Someday she would have to assure Dad that Mom's working had never hurt anything.

As she fell asleep, she wondered why he ever thought it would.

Ryder and Shane loaded the last box into the back of Shane's Explorer, and Taylor squeezed into a space behind Ryder's seat that had been left for her. Josh had gone home with Max earlier in the afternoon, a fact that had excited him and unnerved Taylor.

The men in the front talked shop and tried to include her from time to time, but Taylor was glad for some time to gather her wits. Now that the move was actually taking place, she had second thoughts. She reminded herself that she would have private quarters, that she would still have other patients at the clinic, that many others would be around. Yet in the end, all her thoughts were on Josh and the many hours they would spend alone. And the same old questions haunted her.

How much did she care?

How much did she dare?

When Taylor entered the side door of the ranch, Savannah and Jenny stopped talking with Hannah, and they all stared at her in a way women look when they've been caught gossiping about the person who just walked in. Savannah was the first to step forward, but not before a quick wink at Jenny.

"Here, let me take one of those bags," she said, lightening Taylor's load. "Come on, Jen, let's show her the lucky room." Savannah started up the back stairs that led from the kitchen and Taylor followed, hearing Jenny right behind her.

"Lucky room?" Taylor asked.

"Did I say that?" Savannah kept moving and didn't look back. "I meant pretty room. Actually it's more than a room." She stopped at the threshold and let Taylor precede her.

Stunned at what she saw, Taylor stopped and took in her new surroundings. An old four-poster bed fit snugly between a pair of cross-paned windows, covered in Priscilla-style curtains. A large archway led to a cozy sitting room, complete with a fireplace. Next to her was a private bath, the aroma of scented soaps and potpourri drawing her into the room. She set her load on the floor and pivoted toward the girls.

"It's beautiful." She glanced around, taking in the many antiques and oak-framed watercolors that graced the walls. "I might never want to go home." She chuckled and looked back to the women, whom she caught smiling at each other before they walked in.

Jenny waddled to a window and gazed out. "Brings back many memories...this room."

Savannah deposited Taylor's bag near the closet. "We both stayed in this room when we first visited the ranch. I'm sure you'll be quite comfortable here."

Jenny's gaze turned from the window to Taylor and hung there, in that disconcerting way of hers. "Well, I have to get dinner ready. The men are probably in saying hello to Josh, but they should be up soon with the rest of your things." She left the room and Savannah moved closer, finally pulling Taylor into a quick embrace.

"Welcome to Joeville, Taylor." She stepped back and cupped Taylor's shoulders. "I'm so glad you're here for Josh. I'm sure he'll test your patience, but we're all so grateful you can help."

She couldn't promise anything, she wanted to say. Suddenly she felt as though the pressure of making Josh walk fell squarely on her shoulders, that the entire family expected nothing short of his full recovery.

Ryder and Shane burst through the doorway with the rest of her things and Taylor expelled the breath she'd been holding.

"I'll do my best," she said to Savannah.

Savannah eyed her and smiled. "I know you will."

When Savannah peeked her head in a couple of hours later, Taylor had found places for all her belongings and was shutting the drawer on the nightstand where she'd hidden her mother's journals beneath a scrapbook of family photos.

"Dinner's in five minutes. Hope you've worked up a good appetite. Jenny's outdone herself."

"Thanks. I'll be right down."

Savannah disappeared as quickly as she'd arrived and Taylor dropped onto the side of the bed. The time to face Josh and the task ahead was about to begin. Tonight they would both rest, but tomorrow it would all start—the hard work, the hours together, the nearness of their bodies, the touching that came with the job. She'd had good-looking male patients before, yet this apprehension had never occurred. Was it because Josh was Max's son, and that she owed her mentor so much? Was she worried about letting Max down?

Yes.

She pushed off the comforter and puffed out her cheeks. Who was she kidding? If only it were that simple.

The scent of pot roast and cooked onions rose up to greet her as she descended into the kitchen.

Hannah stopped with her back to the door of the dining room, a tray of iced tea glasses filled to the brim. "Do ya like iced tea, girl? We got other stuff if ya prefer."

Taylor smiled. "Iced tea's perfect. Thank you."

"Well come on, then. Don't be shy. None of 'em will bite ya." Then she cackled. "If they do, they know I'd bite 'em back."

Taylor laughed and followed Hannah, knowing a heart of gold beat beneath the crusty old housekeeper's heavy chest. For a moment she forgot her anxiety.

Until she noticed the only empty seat at the long table. Next to Josh.

And then the Ferris wheel in her stomach started again.

Everyone greeted her as she entered, giving her far too much attention and making it difficult for her to hold eye contact with anyone, until her gaze fell on ten-year-old Billy, his smile so wide that she couldn't help but smile back.

"I think it's way cool you're gonna stay here, Taylor."

She took her seat, avoiding Josh and keeping her focus on Billy, which for the moment felt safer. "Thank you, Billy." He beamed back at her and she knew she had discovered the biggest lady-killer of all the Malones.

Max turned to Hannah as she was about to leave the room. "Won't you join us tonight?"

Hannah waved a chafed hand. "Nah. I gotta plate fixed by the window in the kitchen...where I can watch all my critters. Besides, I'm all tuckered out. Be callin' it an early night soon as I get my fill."

When she'd left, Max looked back at little Billy. "Since you're in such a talkative mood, young man, why don't you lead us in grace tonight?"

His eyes rounded with panic. "Me?"

"Weren't you telling me you learned a new way to pray at Sunday school this week?"

He looked around at the supportive faces and heaved a sigh. "Okay. But we all gotta hold hands first...even the boys." Ryder and Shane, who were sitting next to each other, made a show of grousing, but they took each other's hand and soon a circle had been formed and all heads were bowed.

Taylor took Josh's hand without meeting his gaze. His fingers were long and callused, yet they held hers gently and with confidence. It wasn't the first time a man had held her hand, but as with everything else that involved Joshua Malone, this time was different.

Billy cleared his throat. "The teacher says we should give thanks first before we start asking for stuff."

Ryder nudged him. "Just start, Billy. I think Uncle Shane's falling in love over here."

Savannah reached behind their adopted son and punched her husband's shoulder and Billy began.

"Dear God, thank you for not burning up Uncle Josh with his plane and for sending him home to us at long last. And thank you that there's only twelve days of school left." He paused and Taylor bit her top lip to keep from smiling, wondering what he might say next. "Thank you for taking good care of my mama…and for giving her her own special star. Tell her I see her winking at me every night." He paused and there wasn't a sound except for the crickets outside. "Please give Taylor's mama a star, too. And if you can, maybe her mama and mine could get to be good friends…so when we get there they'll already know all about us."

Josh tightened his hold on Taylor's hand and she managed a swallow, keeping her eyes closed and head bowed.

"And one more thing, Lord, please help Taylor make Uncle Josh walk again. That would make us all real happy. Amen." His words were barely out when he reached for the big bowl of mashed potatoes in front of him, then stopped when no one else moved or spoke. "Did I do it wrong?"

Max recovered first. "It was perfect, Billy. Now get those potatoes moving."

Taylor slipped her hand from beneath Josh's, missing its

warmth as soon as she did. She busied herself spreading her napkin across her lap and waited for Josh to pass her something. He held a basket of fresh-baked biscuits, and she took one without looking up. Before long her plate was filled with more food than she would normally eat in two meals, all of it far surpassing hospital cafeteria food or the quick meals she fixed at home. Yet as hungry as she was, each forkful went down with difficulty. She was an outsider amidst a very close and loving family and again she wondered how Michael and her dad were doing, if they were eating well and keeping up their strength. This was the reason she had lost her appetite, she told herself.

Right. How many different ways would she deny what else was going on? She set her fork down and took a swallow of iced tea, hoping the last bite of beef would dislodge itself and find its way home, all the while reminding herself why she was here. Josh was her patient. Max was her mentor. This was just another job. Like a mantra she repeated the words, shoring herself up for the summer ahead. He'd had an accident and she was feeling sorry for him, but this didn't negate the fact that he was her boss's son. How awkward it would be after...if...

She shifted uncomfortably in her chair and corralled her thoughts. He was a spoiled rich kid who had had everything handed to him on a silver platter. They had about as much in common as molasses and water.

Yes. It was best she held on to that thought.

Jenny placed a piece of chocolate torte in front of Taylor and she dug into it with conviction.

Maybe this handsome cowboy had charmed the pants off half the women for miles around, but he would soon learn that she wasn't interested in his wealth or wit or damnable good looks. It took a lot more than that to woo her.

Yes, sir. He'd met his match this time.

Five

Ever since school had been let out for the summer, Billy had settled into the routine of helping Ryder with chores in the morning, playing with baby Chris until his nap time, then racing down to the clinic to visit with Josh as he worked out with Taylor.

Josh watched Billy bound into the room with an energy that never ceased, and a wave of envy made Josh recall earlier times, times he had taken for granted. Times when walking and running was as easy as breathing.

While Billy stopped to show Taylor a picture he'd drawn, Josh gripped the parallel bars harder, his arms trembling with exhaustion. He would get to the end and drop into his wheelchair if it killed him. And some days, like today, he felt as though it would. He'd been working hard every day for over a month, and still he felt nothing below the waist.

"Hi, Uncle Josh." Billy sat in the wheelchair and spun around a couple of times, thinking it great fun, then returned it in place as Josh grew closer to the end. "Wow! Look at those big muscles in your arms and up there." He pointed to Josh's chest and Josh laughed. "Do you think I could ever look like you?"

Josh sagged into the chair and groaned. "Sure you can." He eyed an approving Taylor. "I know this personal trainer that could help you." He winked, and she rolled her eyes as she always did if he dared flirt with her.

Billy frowned at Taylor. "Do I have to get hurt for you to help me?"

Josh watched her laugh and reassure Billy that wasn't the case. The corners of her eyes and mouth curved upward, little parentheses defining dimples, making her otherwise serious face seem warm and relaxed—an expression he hadn't seen often when it was just the two of them.

Was that what intrigued him so? The challenge of the unattainable? She was easy on the eyes—all that golden blond hair, baby blues and a body that turned heads. Yet just a pretty package wouldn't have him trying so hard. He'd known pretty packages before, and too often they were self-absorbed, and sometimes stumped for an answer when he said hello. Not Taylor. He knew that plenty of brains hid behind that beautiful exterior…and thoughts and dreams and so much more. Still, she revealed nothing to him.

He wondered if she was this intense with all her patients, or if he was the exception. In all their hours together, she hadn't once let him penetrate that glacial facade of hers. He knew it was a facade. Just watching her now with Billy proved that there was warm blood in those cool veins of hers.

What did he have to do to win her trust? Sometimes she would act as though they might become friends, but then she would change before his very eyes, almost as if she'd caught herself slipping. Though he should understand why she wouldn't want to care too much. Who in their right mind would want to start a relationship with a guy who couldn't walk?

Relationship? Now why had he used that word? He meant friendship...didn't he? He wasn't ready for a relationship. Good legs or bad. The fatigue and frustration must be frying his brain.

He sighed and noticed Billy preparing to leave. If only Taylor would relax a little, the way she did with Billy and Max and the rest of the family.

Billy waved goodbye, and Josh said, "See you later, buddy."

Taylor made notes in his chart and he saw that the face she reserved especially for him was firmly back in place. Maybe it was time he learned why, time that he tried harder to make her his friend and break through that barrier she'd erected between them.

She strode toward him in her no-nonsense approach, gripped him beneath the arms and helped lower him to the blue mat alongside his chair. He inhaled her floral perfume, something like lavender, and the familiar scent of her shampoo. He could feel her muscles straining against his, her full breasts flattening against his damp T-shirt. And thoughts of friendship were replaced with something more primal. He could imagine her firm body stretched along the length of him, her long blond hair falling forward on his face, veiling deep, moist kisses he longed to plant on those perfect lips.

He marveled at her strength as she eased him onto his back, and he smiled up at her when she sat back on her heels. Her look was instantly one of contemptuous dismissal. He'd blown it again. His expression must have revealed his true thoughts.

"Can we relax a few minutes and just visit?" *Or you can take your clothes off and roll around on the floor with me.* He didn't have to say it for her reaction to be the same.

Those blue eyes blazed defiance. "I have other patients besides you, you know." She started working one of his legs, bending the knee, raising and lowering it as she had so many times before.

He studied her sure hands a while and let things calm down. Then he braved the question he'd been thinking all morning. "Did I do something wrong?"

She kept working, averting her gaze. "Maybe you don't try as hard as you could some days."

"I wasn't talking about my therapy."

She glanced at him briefly, then moved to the other leg, rivulets of perspiration forming around her hairline.

He tried another approach. "Do you like living here at the ranch?"

She swiped her forehead with the sleeve of her white jacket. "Who wouldn't? It's beautiful." She flashed him a steely look, not breaking stride in her treatment. "Not everyone is so fortunate to live like this."

"Not everything is as perfect as others might think, either," he shot. He saw a small crack in her veneer and he raised up on his elbows. "Money can't buy everything, Taylor."

"Obviously." A beat passed before she glanced at him. "I—I'm sorry. I wasn't referring to—" She was staring at his legs now and looking embarrassed.

"I know you weren't." He grabbed her hand and held it still. "But what *were* you referring to?"

She tried to free her hand but he wouldn't let go. She shrugged. "Nothing in particular."

"Would you just stop and look at me a minute. Please?"

Her head was slow in coming around, but she finally met his gaze.

"Why don't you like me, Taylor? What have I ever done to you?"

She blinked and started to look away, but when he tugged at her wrist, she looked back.

"Who said I didn't like you?"

"Do you?"

She averted her gaze, and he tugged her back again.

"Tell me. Do you?"

She opened her mouth then closed it as if she might choke on the words.

Damn. He hadn't meant to back her into a corner, to act like a bully. He let out a weary sigh. If he was sincere in wanting to win her over, there had to be a better approach.

"I can be a real jerk sometimes, can't I?" He eyed her, and at last she rewarded him with a small smile. "Look...I really appreciate all your help and patience with me. I know I haven't always been the easiest patient. It's just that...well, all this time we've spent together...I was hoping we could get to know each other better."

He saw a light pink tinge creeping up her neck, which surprised and encouraged him. "There was something I was hoping you'd talk to me about, but you haven't mentioned the subject once."

He let go of her wrist and she sat back, a frown dimpling the space between her brows. "And what subject might that be?"

He paused, afraid of losing the small ground he'd gained, forging ahead, anyway. "Your mother."

She lowered her head and started playing with a chipped nail. There was so much pain on her face that he thought she might cry. But she didn't. She sucked it in and said nothing.

He pushed on. "We talked a little about her that day I took you to the airport." She looked as though she were ready to run from the room, yet she sat very still. "I know what it's like to lose a mother. And I also know I didn't talk about it for years and it ate a hole in me. I—I still haven't...very much."

Taylor looked him in the eye at last and he saw the moisture brimming above her lower lashes.

"I didn't mean to make you blue," he whispered. He reached out to touch her, but she was too far away from him. "I just thought that...well...if you ever needed to talk, I wanted you to know I was here." He shrugged, trying to ease out of an area he hadn't planned to approach. "We could reminisce about the good times with our moms. It doesn't have to be all sad."

She bit her bottom lip, fighting valiantly for control. Gone were the games she'd been playing with him, at least for now. And in that brief silent moment, he thought he cared more about this woman kneeling beside him than any he'd ever met.

She sniffed once, then started massaging his leg again. They finished the session without another word, but Josh could see the change behind Taylor's eyes. She wasn't angry or defiant now. Something was churning behind those big baby blues.

If only he knew what.

After supper Taylor helped Jenny and Savannah with dishes, letting the pair carry the conversation, her mind drifting back to her time with Josh earlier. She wished she *could* talk with him about her mother. She knew talking with anyone about her loss would help. And Josh would certainly understand how she felt.

So why did she always hold back with him? Because professionalism dictated she keep a distance from her patients? Possibly. But not likely.

She pictured Josh's handsome face, as she had so often lately when they weren't together, and her heartbeat quickened. Their time together was only intensifying an attraction she found more and more difficult to control, which left her asking the same tired questions. Did she have to control her feelings for Josh? Were they real or only an illusion? Some bizarre extension of her mother's feelings for Max? If only she could be certain which. She felt so vulnerable and full of doubts about everything these days.

Jenny said good-night and Savannah followed her down the hall, leaving Taylor alone with her thoughts as she trudged up the back stairs. The windows had been open all day, and she tugged them closed. The sun was lower in the sky, and a damp spring chill had filled the room.

A long-nosed butane lighter rested on one end of the mantel in the sitting room. She went to it and started the gas logs. Then, shedding her clothes and slipping into her robe, she removed a journal from the nightstand and crossed to the small love seat in front of the blue-tinged flames and sat down with a heavy sigh. *Oh, Mama, I miss you so. If only you were here to counsel me about Josh. What would you say?* She rubbed her eyes with the back of her hand, then picked up the calico-covered book and continued where she had left off.

I got my hair cut and styled yesterday and bought some new makeup while I was out. I told myself it was good for my late-winter blahs, that it would perk me up. But it's getting harder to deceive myself these days. The bald truth is that I wanted Max to notice the change and say something—which he did, of course. He seems to notice every little thing, and I feel like a schoolgirl when he does. We seem to be thrown together for more and more patients these days. We work well as a team and someone must have noticed. I hope that's all anyone noticed. There's such a heat that comes over me when I'm near him, I wonder if I'm blushing or if anyone can tell how much I enjoy the nearness of him, or if they catch the way his gaze lingers on mine a little too long.

A part of me says I should stop these fantasies gathering speed in the back of my head. Then I tell myself he'll be going back to Montana soon, and that will be that. In a way I wish he'd leave tomorrow, but then I feel this big empty void and want to cry.

I find John staring at me at the oddest times these days, and I wonder if he can read my mind. I've been making his favorite meals and asking about his latest carpentry jobs, trying to assure him I care. He's such

a good man. Kind and gentle and true. Just the way
he was when we married—which only increases my
guilt.

I can still remember that day as if it were yesterday.
An inner voice warned me something was missing.
Why didn't I listen? And how do I fix things now?

Just a little longer and Max will be gone and my
life will return to normal. I adjusted before when he
left. I can do it again. But why, oh, why did he have
to come back?

Tonight I looked at my precious angel asleep in her
bed, and I prayed she will grow up to be stronger and
more patient than her mother, that she will wait for
that special man—not just a good man, but one who
leaves her short of breath, one who makes her heart
sing with pure joy. God forgive me for even thinking
this.

I pray she finds a man like Max.

Taylor set the journal aside and stared into the fire. She'd
known about her mother's and Max's mutual respect and
friendship, but these pages spoke of much more. How much
more she wasn't sure she wanted to know.

With a sense of foreboding, Taylor put the book away
and slipped between the sheets. Could Mom have had an
affair with Max? Is that why the day before she died she'd
said "Please don't hate me"?

She closed her eyes and shook her head. No. Mom would
have been true to her vows, no matter how enormous the
temptation, no matter how strong her feelings for Max.

It seemed strange thinking of her mother lusting after
anyone, even Dad. She was a passionate person on many
levels so it shouldn't come as a total surprise. But Max?
Her mentor and friend?

Taylor saw Max's handsome face in her mind's eye. He
must have been something else when he was younger. Possibly as rakish as…as…

Josh.

I pray she will grow up to be stronger and more patient than her mother, that she will wait for that special man—not just a good man, but one who leaves her short of breath, one who makes her heart sing with pure joy.

Taylor rolled on her side and punched the pillow. This was ridiculous. It wasn't like her to indulge in such romantic fantasies. To even *consider* that she and Josh could satisfy their parents' unrequited love was insane. That's all she was doing, wasn't it?

She turned over and stared into the darkness, not certain of anything anymore.

Josh's behavior during therapy the following week made it easier for Taylor to hold her feelings in check. Not only was he irritable, but he was often late, or he would use his cell phone to call the farm and talk to the help about his crops. Anything rather than focus on the problem at hand.

And the problem was that his condition wasn't improving, and that his spirits were declining each day.

It didn't help when his brothers made daily visits and talked of the upcoming cattle drive, an event Josh said he hadn't missed in nearly twenty years. Ryder and Shane offered to rig something up in a wagon so Josh could join them, but this only made him angrier.

"I'd be more trouble than I was worth. Thanks, but no thanks. You guys go ahead. Leave the gimp behind."

Taylor watched the exchange between the brothers, feeling disheartened herself. She'd done everything in her power to bring life back into Josh's legs, but as yet, nothing had worked.

Still, it wasn't like Josh to indulge in self-pity. Anger, frustration, she understood. But this recent pattern of self-deprecation was not a good sign. She'd seen it before. When a patient had given up. As sympathetic as she was to the situation, she wasn't about to encourage Josh's sense of hopelessness. Better that he should be angry.

Shane turned to Taylor as he and Ryder started to leave. "How do you put up with this guy day in and day out?"

He was trying to sound light, but Taylor remembered what Max had told her: Shane felt guilty for his brother's paralysis, and no one could convince him otherwise.

Taylor kneaded Josh's thigh harder and said, "Oh, I've worked with bigger jerks than your brother." She glanced at him and saw no humor, only a look of loathing. "Some people have just had it too easy all their lives. They don't know what *real* work is all about."

Josh swatted her hand away. "That does it." His jaw muscles were working double time. She had pressed too far. "I've had enough of this crap for one day. Help me into the chair."

Taylor brought his wheelchair around and locked the wheels. "Here you go. Help yourself." With that, she joined the openmouthed brothers in the doorway, hooked their elbows and walked them away from the clinic.

When they were out of earshot, Shane asked, "Don't you think you're being a little hard on him?"

Taylor stopped and shared a look between their worried faces. "He's giving up. We can't let him do that." Awareness started to penetrate their frowns. "Amazing things can happen in cases like Josh's...when properly motivated."

Ryder chuckled. "You mean—when properly pissed off."

Taylor smiled and nodded. "You could say that."

Yet Josh wasn't like most of Taylor's patients. He was headstrong and didn't take guff from anyone. When he finally managed to pull himself into his chair, he wheeled around the corner and found his father on the phone.

Max eyed him curiously and ended the conversation soon after. "What's up, son?"

"I want to move back to the farm. The men need me." Max raised an eyebrow and Josh continued. "It would be easier to run things from there. Besides, it feels more like home." He let out a long breath and slowed down. "I mean...I'm sorry, Dad. I don't mean to sound ungrateful, it's just that—"

Max came around his desk and leaned against it. "I understand, Josh. You worked hard on that old house...it's your home now. But you can't stay out there alone. Not yet."

"I got it all worked out. Hank and the others can take turns looking in on me, and I'll keep my cell phone nearby...just in case. I need to fend for myself, Dad." He needed to get away from Taylor, too. He'd done all he could to make her more than his therapist. And the end result was as successful as his attempts to walk—which, now that he thought about it, was probably for the best. If he was going to spend his life in this chair, there was no point in trying to get closer to Taylor or any woman.

"I don't suppose I could talk you into waiting a while longer."

Josh shook his head. "I'd like to do it today." He could see the decision warring in his father's eyes and it was some time before he spoke again. But then his voice was firm and decisive.

"Okay, son. I'll talk to your brothers about helping with the move and getting you settled in. Take a couple days off. But then I'm sending Taylor over to resume your therapy." Josh started to protest, but his father wouldn't allow it. "We'll have to leave equipment here for the other patients, but we can move some over to your place and set it up in the parlor for you."

"Dad—"

"There's no point arguing, Joshua. I don't care how old

you are, I'm still your father. And in case you've forgotten, I'm still a doctor. I know what has to be done.''

Josh lowered his head, the fight seeping out of him. The accident had cost him more than the use of his legs; it had cost him his freedom, his independence. And that he hated most.

Josh slanted a frustrated glare at his father, then turned his chair around and wheeled out of the room.

Max watched Josh go and his heart ached. If he could give his own legs in order to see his son walk again, he would. Yet tough times demanded tough decisions. Plus he *did* know what had to be done. And what better person to do it than Taylor? Angela's skilled and beautiful daughter.

How strange that Taylor would be the one here for Josh now. Was this God's way of saying Max Malone was forgiven? That the sins of the father wouldn't be revisited on the son? Or might Josh never walk again and Taylor leave? If so, neither would have the chance to truly know what life could hold had they stayed together.

As had been the case for another couple so long ago.

Max sauntered to the window and tried to take in the MoJoe Mountains and the miles of rolling fields in between. The view usually brought peace and serenity to his hectic days.

Today he didn't even see it.

All he could see was the warm smile of a young woman who had meant the world to him. A woman who was lost to him now and forever.

A woman he couldn't even grieve for when anyone was watching.

Six

Josh and Hank huddled at the kitchen table, going over figures from wheat sales and a list of jobs to be done. Profits weren't even close to projections, the fire from the crash having leveled nearly a quarter of the fields. Thankfully the blaze had been contained far from the farmhouse.

"Somethin's wrong with the irrigation in the southwest corner," Hank said, leaning back in his chair.

"What happened to the unit that was in the fire?"

"It didn't get fried like the wheat, but it still don't work. Any chance a gettin' a new one?"

They had to cut corners where they could. The new plane was supposed to have been covered by selling the old one plus healthy wheat revenues. Now money was tight. His, anyway. And he'd hoped never to ask his dad for help, especially since he'd never been too keen on the idea of a rancher's son growing crops. Josh yawned and stretched, trying to reduce the tension in his back and shoulders.

"Why don't you take another look at the one from the fire. See if there are any usable parts you can cannibalize."

There was a quick rap on the side door before Ryder and Shane burst in, each carrying a workout bar.

Josh groaned and pointed. "In the parlor. But you're going to have to move some furniture out of the way first."

"Can a guy get a beer around this joint?" Ryder called over his shoulder.

"Work first, beer later," Josh said, not meaning to take out his frustration on his brothers.

Shane called out from the parlor as the pair rearranged the room. "Jenny's been cooking up a storm. Got a big box outside. Everything freezer-wrapped and labeled."

Hank stood to leave, rotating the rim of his Stetson in his hands in front of him and looking eager to return to work. "Will that be all, boss?"

Josh stretched out his hand, and Hank shook it firmly. "Thanks, Hank. Don't know what I would have—"

Hank held up a palm, seeming embarrassed. "Don't mention it. I'll check in on ya later."

Shane and Ryder were right on his heels as he left, getting another load from Ryder's truck. The door opened again and Josh was about to speak when Taylor blew in, her attitude barely fitting through the doorway.

She was hot. And he didn't think it was from wanting to jump his bones, either. At least not in any fun way. He swallowed a chuckle and watched. The intervening days may have cooled his temper somewhat, but something had definitely doused hers with a full can of kerosene.

Josh watched her storm past him to the parlor and heard the loud clang of metal as she made adjustments to the bars. He wondered if saying hello would be enough to make her explode.

Shane and Ryder carried in more boxes than he could imagine were needed and disappeared into the next room. As soon as Jenny's goodies were stashed in the refrigerator, the men looked at Taylor, then Ryder said, "Well, think

I'll grab that beer at home. We'll leave you two to your work. See you around.'' He tipped his hat to Taylor, who Josh noticed didn't smile, and then they left. Ran away was more like it. They took off down the drive like a pair of scared rabbits, gravel crunching beneath the tires, a cloud of dust drifting back toward the kitchen window.

Josh looked from the truck to Taylor, trying to puzzle it out. What did they know that he didn't? Something more than resuming his therapy was in the wind, and he was determined to find out exactly what it was.

Taylor was standing in front of the bay window in the parlor, her arms folded tightly across her chest. Furniture, equipment and boxes haphazardly blocking a path between them. Light streaked through her windblown, fair hair, and the glare of the setting sun behind her left him temporarily blinded to the features of her face. Yet there was no mistaking the anger in her posture and stony silence.

''Now what?'' he asked when he couldn't stand the quiet another second.

''Now I have to find a bedroom and put these boxes away.'' She flung out her arms indicating the mess around her, and then slapped her thighs in disgusted resignation.

''I'm confused,'' he said. She ignored him and picked up a box. ''I thought we were going to set up in here.''

She brushed passed him. ''We are.'' Behind him she stopped and asked, ''Where's the guest room?''

He spun his chair around and cocked his head. ''Why?''

''So I can take a nap,'' she snapped. ''Hurry up. This box weighs a ton.''

''You're not planning to—''

''Move in? That's the plan. Up or down?''

''Up,'' he said, not believing his ears. She started for the stairs. ''Whose bright idea was this?''

''Certainly not mine! Talk to your dad.''

He yelled up the stairwell. ''I certainly will.''

He cranked one wheel of his chair and looked at the

chaos in his once-well-ordered home. And then he thought of the chaos traipsing around upstairs.

How could his father do this to him? Taylor under the same roof? Alone with him, day after day? He thought he'd made it perfectly clear that he needed his space. He turned around and headed for the kitchen phone, wishing he could kick something instead.

Frustrated, he swore at the sounds overhead, and suddenly the mess in the parlor seemed the least of his worries.

Taylor paced down the hall, pausing in each doorway—office, bathroom...

She stopped at the end of the hall, and her mouth dropped open.

In the last room an antique maple dresser dominated one wall and a matching carved headboard graced a tall double bed, a huge downy comforter drawing her closer. Alongside the bed was a small step stool, one she would need if she didn't want to take a running start and jump into its inviting center—which at this moment seemed very appealing.

She set the box down next to a well-preserved hope chest at the foot of the bed and turned slowly, taking in her new surroundings. A watercolor of the MoJoes hung on one wall, tall ivory candles in sconces on either side. An overstuffed wing chair and ottoman sat at an angle in one corner next to the multipaned windows, a bearskin rug covering the hardwood floor between herself and the chair. She crossed to it, walking around the rug, and tested the seat gingerly, gazing around in disbelief. Maybe she hated being coerced into staying here, but she loved this room. It was so well put together, all in earth tones, so peaceful and harmonious, so...so...

Unlike Joshua Malone.

Or was it?

She rotated her neck, trying to get the kinks out of it, then leaned back and closed her eyes. Slowly she inhaled and exhaled until she felt herself relax.

Today was the first time she could ever remember arguing with Max. He had never done anything before that resembled pulling rank. He'd always guided, suggested, encouraged. This time when she'd said no to him, he'd simply stared at her, his eyes saying "after all I've done for you?" as surely as if he'd spoken the words. Max had a reputation at the hospital as a man used to getting his way, but she'd never seen that side of him. She hoped she never would again.

Still, she did owe him. Big-time. In the past, whenever classes she'd wanted were full, he'd always found her a seat; when she hadn't been getting enough hours of work to make ends meet, he would help her find a way.

As the anger seeped from her, guilt reared its ugly head. Not only was Josh Max's son, he was a man without the use of his legs. What was she moaning about? So what if she found him spoiled, self-centered, difficult...and *almost* irresistible.

That was it, wasn't it? That was the part that worried her most.

Her hormones were raging, and she wasn't used to fighting for control.

But hadn't Josh tried everything in his power to befriend her? Did she mistrust her emotions so much that she couldn't stop there?

And while she was at it, what exactly did she want? Lately she'd been so busy running back and forth between her patients in Bozeman and the ranch, plus working overtime with Josh, that she hadn't had a moment to think of the future. Before all this, besides her career, she'd always assumed there would be a husband and children eventually—when the right man came along. A man like her father. And each time she entertained the idea of Josh fitting those shoes, he had always come up lacking.

Yet now, looking around the warm home he'd carved out for himself, she wondered if maybe Josh was more like her father than she gave him credit for. How much of the remodeling did Josh actually do? She'd never had occasion to even drive near this place, and she'd been so angry when she walked in, she hadn't noticed much of the downstairs. She closed her eyes and rested her head against the back of the chair.

Maybe it was time to cut him a little slack.

From the bottom of the steps, Josh shouted up to her. "Are you *really* taking a nap or are you going to get this crap out of my way?"

Taylor pushed out of the chair and prayed for God to give her strength. This man wasn't going to make things easy.

The steam she'd been able to shed seemed transferred to Josh's face when she returned to the parlor for another box. Between trips up and down the stairs, she did her best not to notice his foul mood, holding tight to her earlier hope that things between them could change. But finally, after the last load and a half-dozen more of his gibes, her patience flew out the window along with all her good intentions.

"Look, why don't you work off some of that steam on the bars. Maybe it will help you relax." And me, too. This man was driving her crazy.

The last thing Josh wanted to do tonight, or any night, was work on the bars, or anything, as far as that goes. Nights were for sitting in front of the open hearth, for listening to the crickets or a coyote in full voice, for contemplating one's navel, if all else failed. Anything but work.

But there was this blond firestorm of energy unrolling the blue mat beneath those damnable bars that he had come to hate. And she wasn't about to take no for an answer.

"Do you want to change clothes first?" she asked.

He shot her his best if-looks-could-kill glare, then unbuttoned his shirt and tossed it aside, leaving him in only a T-shirt and jeans, his feet already bare. "Okay. I'll give it fifteen minutes. Then will you leave me alone?"

She flashed him what looked like a sincere smile, which stunned him.

"Until morning—when it's time for your next session."

"Then let's get this over with. I have more productive things to do." Such as staring out the window, watching and listening to the wilderness. Things this driven woman couldn't possibly understand. Yet she still smiled. Hmm. What could she be up to now?

When the fifteen minutes passed, she eased him into his chair and said, "Good job."

He frowned, trying to remember if he'd ever heard those two words pass her lips before.

"Need me to help you with...well, anything...before I call it a night?"

"Hank will be by in a while, but thanks."

"Want something to drink while you wait?"

Who was this woman? "A cold beer might taste good." She started for the kitchen, glancing around his home as she went. "Don't need a glass," he called after her.

A moment later she handed him a can, gave a shoulder-high little wave that made his heart race, then ascended the stairs.

"See you in the morning," she said.

Taylor propped a couple of goose down pillows behind her back and thought about the evening. They hadn't talked about anything significant, but it had been a pleasant enough time. Had she been such a grump before that when she finally acted nice to him it left him looking like a deer caught in the headlights?

Probably so.

Well, all that was about to change. She owed it to Max to try harder. She wanted complete recovery for Josh—the same as she did for all her other patients. In that regard, Josh was no different.

Right. She'd never been much of a liar, not even to herself. But if he wasn't simply a patient to her, what was he?

She plumped the pillows behind her and looked for a distraction, anything to take her mind off the man downstairs and the confusion he generated.

In the third unpacked box she opened, she found her mother's journal, crawled back into bed and searched for the last line she had read: "I pray she finds a man like Max."

Slowly, Taylor shut the book and set it aside. Her heart beat erratically as she closed her eyes, suddenly too tired to focus on the page, her thoughts a jumble.

Josh wasn't what she would call a carbon copy of his father, but he did possess Max's good looks and charm.

And this house! She wasn't what she considered a materialistic person, but she enjoyed beauty wherever she found it. She eyed the coved ceilings and six-panel hardwood doors, finally shaking her head. For some reason she'd expected Josh's home to be some brand-new contemporary monstrosity. What a pleasant surprise this was. And with this discovery she felt her control plummeting to a new low.

She slid deeper under the covers, amazed at how comfortable she felt with her new surroundings. For the moment, at least, she didn't even fight it.

Perhaps tomorrow she would ask Josh to tell her the story of this house—who had lived here before, who had restored it, how he'd come to live here instead of at the ranch. It would give them a safe topic. Besides, she truly wanted to know.

As sleep started to overtake her, she snuggled deeper under the down comforter and had the strangest sensation...home...she felt as though she was finally home....

But the next day only brought frustration and no forward progress. And with each passing day, Josh became more irritable, no longer apologizing for barking at Taylor when he grew impatient. She'd seen this behavior often enough with other patients, yet she'd foolishly allowed herself to think Josh might be different.

So she retreated behind her job, burying her questions about the house and any silly notion that Josh might ever become more than a patient. The girls on campus probably had him pegged right.

Joshua Malone wanted only one thing: another notch on his bedpost.

What surprised her was the hurt and disappointment that accompanied this line of thinking. She hadn't realized how much she'd wanted him to prove her wrong.

In part, she thought, her mother's journal had contributed to this feeling. If only Mom were here today. Taylor would hold her tight and assure her she was not hated for her secret, as she had so feared before she died.

Mom was a vital, passionate woman, a woman who sacrificed much to make a loving home for all of them. As much as Taylor loved her father, she could see now that there were many differences between her parents. Both were good people, yet each quite unique. And from what Taylor had read these past few weeks, she knew Max was more like her mother. He seemed calm and controlled with patients, staff and herself, but through Mom's eyes Taylor saw the man beneath.

Max lost a patient this afternoon. I found him alone in the lounge, standing in front of the window, his head bent low. I thought maybe I should leave, but something drew me closer. I didn't know the words to comfort him so I simply stood beside him, feeling his pain as though it were my own.

I longed to reach over and take his hand in mine. His nearness felt like a magnet and as always it was excruciating not to touch him. Still, I knew if I did that he would know—if he doesn't already—how very much I care for him, how I ache for him to take me in his arms and never let me go.

I think he must have sensed this when he turned from the window and gazed at me. There was sadness in his eyes, and I didn't think it was only his lost patient he was thinking of at that moment.

Sometimes I think I will go mad—keeping these feelings deep inside. Thank God for Taylor when I get home each night. We play and laugh and I pour out all the love I've been suppressing.

John is such a good man. Though my body has remained faithful to him, my mind and heart have betrayed him many times. Maybe next week, when Max returns to Montana, I will be able to lock away my feelings and recommit to John.

Please, God, give me the strength to say goodbye to Max and be the kind of wife John deserves.

The oddest thing was happening to Taylor: the more she read how much Mom had wanted Max, the more she was drawn to Josh.

And more and more lately, as the attraction intensified, she wished her mother was here for one of those long talks they used to have.

What would she think about Josh? Would she say "Follow your heart"? Or would she worry how this would hurt Dad? If he even knew. If he didn't, how could he? There were so many questions that only her mother could answer.

And what about Josh's reputation with women? She had yet to hear of anything long-lasting.

Taylor tossed throughout the night, dreaming of Josh in the few minutes of real sleep she got. When the alarm sounded, she bounded out of bed, angry with herself for allowing such feelings of powerlessness to overcome her. If Mom could control herself, so could she.

She showered and dressed quickly, trying to ignore that pesky inner voice of hers that kept saying *Yes, but your mother was married. What's your excuse?*

She left her room and strode toward the stairs, telling herself all she had to do was work harder and ignore that pesky voice. But it got the last word.

How much longer can you ignore your feelings?

Seven

Late Friday afternoon of the following week, Josh could feel the last threads of civility about to snap. Anyone within striking range was fair game for his fury. And there was no doubt what had brought him to this breaking point: he had biceps to die for, but his legs were still useless.

Perhaps they always would be, he thought, inching along the hated bars as Taylor watched. He'd never considered himself a quitter, but maybe it was time to face reality and admit that this was as good as it was going to get.

"This isn't working," he said between clenched teeth.

"*You're* not working!"

The phone rang and she started for it.

He yelled, "Let it ring."

Taylor turned on her heel and came back to him, stopping at the end of the bars, gripping them hard with white-knuckled fists. He could see she was struggling for control, too. But he didn't care. Maybe a good fight would make him feel better. All this bottled up frustration was sending him around the bend and he had a feeling that her rejection of him was as much the cause as his useless legs. Finally, when the ringing stopped, Taylor stepped between the bars and moved closer for the confrontation that he could see in her eyes.

"Where's your commitment, Joshua Malone?" There was a mocking sarcasm in her voice that grated on his already frazzled nerves. Was she purposefully egging him on? Then again, why did he care? He was begging for a fight, anyway. Inside he smiled. Whatever she was up to, she'd better be ready; she wasn't going to win this one.

"Where's yours, Taylor Phillips?" he said, jutting out his chin, driving his face dangerously close to hers.

"What do you mean 'Where's yours?'" Instead of backing away, she shifted forward aggressively.

"*Commitment!* I don't think you understand the meaning of the word."

"Huh! And look who's calling the kettle black! What exactly are you committed to, oh, righteous one?"

He ground his teeth. "Many things. Family, for one."

"Me, too. What else?" She shifted her weight to the opposite leg.

"My work."

"Me, too."

"My faith in God…through good times and bad."

She cocked her head and narrowed her eyes. "Really? I hadn't noticed." She folded her arms and stared at him. "But me, too." Her gaze drifted off, then on a sigh, she eyed him again. "This contest is growing tiresome. Why don't you cut to the chase—tell me what you're really thinking…tell me one thing you're committed to that you think I'm not."

At last she'd asked the right question. Now he would win.

He tried not to act smug when he answered. "Allowing something to develop between us." He noticed the sudden discomfort on Taylor's face and knew she wasn't going to

squirm her way out this time. When she said nothing, he
added. "And to let myself trust you...to know that you're
the kind of person who would never betray that trust. *That's*
what else I'm committed to."

Something she apparently was not, since she didn't say
"me, too." And in that instant he realized winning wasn't
bringing him the pleasure and release he had hoped for.
Instead, he wished that she would say something, anything,
to prove him wrong.

But what she did next caught him completely off guard.
She closed the small space between them, her gaze fixed
on his lips. With lightning speed, she clasped his face between her strong fingers and pressed her mouth to his. The
kiss was quick and hard and punishing.

"You haven't a clue how I feel, Joshua Malone."

The heat he felt creeping up his neck had nothing to do
with the past hour of workout. In the blink of an eye everything had changed. "Then tell me," he said. "How *do*
you feel?"

She inched back a little and wrinkled her forehead.
"Confused."

"About...?"

"Whether I want to be your friend or—"

"Or...?"

"Much more." She searched his face as if hoping to find
a clue to the right answer.

"I—I..."

With a roll of her eyes, she impatiently clutched his head
in her hands once more. "Why don't you just shut up and
kiss me?"

He opened his lips in surprise and her mouth covered his
again, this time in no hurry. He felt her tongue plunge inside, its warmth and moisture making him forget all else.
He returned her kiss with an urgency he never remembered
feeling. If only he could let go of the bars and wrap his
arms around her. She tilted her head and found a better

angle, exploring the recesses of his mouth, her breathing as ragged as his own.

Finally she broke their kiss and thrust her arms under his, gently lowering him to the mat below. He reached out for her, wanting to pull her down onto him, but she stood abruptly, her gaze never leaving his. With meticulous pacing, she removed her jacket, then her top and everything else, not seeming shy or embarrassed as he would have expected, but deliberately taunting him.

He locked his fingers behind his head and enjoyed the show, for once not wanting to say a word. Except for the beating of his heart, the room was perfectly still, a gentle breeze tickling a few branches near the open window near his head.

When she stood naked at his feet, her blue eyes turned dark and she seemed to hesitate for the slightest of moments. He held out his arms for her to come to him, but she shook her head from side to side and whispered, "Not yet."

As slowly as she had undressed herself, she continued with him, all with the same precision. Each arm was tugged free and his T-shirt passed over his face. She unbuckled his belt and he closed his eyes. God how he wanted this woman. If only he could feel something, if only he could love her the way he pictured it in his mind.

She tugged off his jeans and shorts and then at last she spread herself over the length of him. He opened his eyes and started to speak, but she pressed a finger to his lips and made a soft shushing sound.

Slowly she turned her attention to his neck, planting soft little kisses everywhere, until she reached his ear. Her tongue moved constantly, the feel and sound of it leaving him breathless. At last her mouth returned to his and it was all he could do not to hurt her as he matched the hunger in her lips and tongue. His hands scurried over her back, pulling her closer and closer. Her nipples rubbed the moist hair of his chest, and he groaned into her mouth. If only he could slip inside her and complete the act his brain cried out for. If only he could bring her as much pleasure as she was showering on him. He slid his hand down her thigh and then tunneled between her legs, not surprised to find hot moisture when his fingers slipped inside her.

She broke their kiss and straddled him now, riding his hand, her head tipped back and lips parted. He worked his fingers, determined to bring her to completion. She groaned and squirmed over him until finally he felt her quiver and a rush of hot liquid washed through his fingers.

She stared at him, her breathing still labored. He expected her to snuggle next to him or maybe kiss him, but when he saw a slow smile curve her lips and her right arm begin to move, he glanced down at her hand.

She was stroking him ever so lightly. He couldn't feel it, but he could see it. He stared in shocked disbelief. A bubble of laughter emerged from deep in his throat. "Well, I'll be damned."

She kept stroking and he watched her—the most erotic vision he had ever seen. Slowly, she positioned herself over his rigid shaft and lowered herself, inch by miraculous inch. When she had filled herself with him, she ground her hips and closed her eyes, then dropped to his damp body and claimed his mouth once again.

His senses swam and he longed to rise up and meet her thrusts. But he held her tight to him and told her with his lips and arms how much she and this moment meant to him.

Her movements grew faster and their breathing came in gulps. Finally she shuddered into his embrace, her raspy voice whispering in his ears, "Oh, Josh, Josh." And at long last she slumped against him.

He kissed her neck and tasted her salt, holding her tight and never wanting to let her go. What a gift she had given him. He didn't know...he thought he would never...

Taylor slid to his side and cuddled her head in the crook of his arm, her own arm draped over his chest, a knee bent over his thigh. He closed his eyes and savored the moment, wishing it never had to end. In his wildest dreams he never would have imagined this magical afternoon.

They lay there for the longest time, the sun slipping lower behind the MoJoes, and still they didn't speak. He wondered what she was thinking, if she was regretting her impulsiveness already. If she was, he didn't want to know, so he didn't move or make a sound. He listened to the horses whinnying in the stable and remembered that Hank would be stopping by soon. What would the old guy think if he caught them like this? He smiled and was just about to warn Taylor of the hour, when he heard tires crunching over the gravel drive.

Taylor sat up with a start, scrambling first for her own clothes, then finding his shorts and T-shirt. She stared at his jeans in her hands, then hurled them onto a chair, apparently deciding they would take too long to put on.

Josh sat up and Taylor hoisted him back onto the bars, her long blond hair uncharacteristically tousled, her face flushed.

The kitchen door opened and closed and boots ambled across the plank flooring. Taylor stood with her back to the visitor while Josh looked around her shoulder and grinned. "Shane! What brings you here?"

Josh followed Shane's gaze as it traveled from the jeans on the chair to the pair supposedly working at the bars. Unable to wipe the grin off his face, Josh offered a weak explanation. "Been working out really hard today. Got a little hot in here."

He glanced at Taylor's wide-eyed look and knew she was begging him not to spill the beans. "Guess this isn't the first time a physical therapist saw a patient in his under-wear."

Shane folded his arms, leaned against the wall and let a shadow of a smile cross his face. "Probably not."

"So what can I do for you?" And how many more ways do I have to hint that your timing stinks?

"Jenny made a great pot roast tonight and wanted me to drop off dinner for you two." His smiled widened. "I'll leave it in the kitchen and be on my way." He paused. "Oh, and Taylor...Jen and Savannah were hoping you would have time to visit with them tomorrow. They've got something up their sleeves. I'm not sure what."

"Okay," she said, her back still to him.

Shane chuckled softly, walked toward the kitchen and called back to Josh. "Just remember, little bro. Paybacks are hell."

The side door opened and closed, and the pair in the parlor eyed each other.

"What did he mean by that?" Taylor asked.

Josh debated whether to tell her the truth, but in the end he did. "Well, before I moved out here, Jenny and Shane got stranded here overnight in a snowstorm. When I arrived the next morning, I caught them moving a mattress from in front of the fireplace, back to the bedroom. They acted as if nothing had happened, but...well..."

Taylor got the wheelchair, positioned it behind him, and he dropped into it with a whoosh. "I get the picture," she said curtly, not sounding as if she found any amusement in the story. She wheeled him to the kitchen where the aroma of cooked onions seeped from beneath the foil-wrapped roast. "Would you like me to dish you up a plate?"

He shook his head, not ready to eat, although he was famished.

"Then, I think I'll go upstairs. I'm not very hungry."

He glanced over his shoulder at her, puzzled by this sudden change. Sure, she was embarrassed by Shane barging in the way he had. But now it was just the two of them. And they had just made love. He had hoped they would sit in front of the fire and hold hands, maybe talk all night...or maybe even...

"Taylor?" He spun his chair around and faced her. "What's wrong? Talk to me."

She stared at the floor in front of him, her bottom lip

starting to quiver. "I'm sorry. I've never done such a thing—"

"Do you hear me complaining?" He hoped she would smile, just a little, but she wouldn't even meet his gaze.

"D-do you need anything before I go up?"

An explanation would be nice. But he could see that wasn't forthcoming. At least not tonight. He lowered his voice, not hiding his disappointment. "No. Hank should be here soon."

"I—" She turned suddenly and he suspected she was crying.

"It's okay, Taylor," he said, without much heart. "I'll see you in the morning." And maybe then you can tell me what's wrong.

He listened to her light footfalls on the stairs and across the hallway overhead, and then heard the door to her room closing.

He'd never pretended to be an expert on women, but this one truly had him stumped. He left the kitchen, paused at the foot of the stairs and glanced up. Who was the real Taylor Phillips?

At first she'd acted as though she disliked him. From there she'd moved to tolerance, resisting his attempts at friendship. Then, pow! She seduces him without batting an eye. And now? Now she won't even hold his gaze or discuss what just happened between them.

What on earth was behind this peculiar behavior? He would like to think she would tell him in the morning, but with Taylor, nothing was predictable and nothing was that simple.

Taylor fought the urge to fling the journal through the window. Instead she stuffed it in the nightstand drawer and slammed it shut so hard that the lamp on top teetered and she had to grab it before it fell.

Oh, Mama, what have I done? You were so strong and I was so weak.

She slumped on the bed, her mind and heart a whirl of conflicting thoughts and feelings. It had seemed right at the moment. And there was no denying that the sex was good. Better than good. But that was the problem; it was sex, not love. Wasn't it? She was so confused.

She clasped her ears and squeezed her eyes shut, but the questions wouldn't stop. Could she be in love with this man? Or had the daughter simply absorbed the mother's frustration so acutely that she couldn't resist the Malone charm and attraction another moment?

And what attraction was she acting on? Her mother's for Max? Or her own for Josh?

She flopped back spread-eagle and wished she was alone in the house. A good primal scream would feel good about now. But she could hear Hank below with Josh, so she took long, deep breaths and let them out slowly, trying to still the panic in her chest.

It didn't work.

She felt as if she were on a train without brakes. Things had happened so fast, and she felt herself careening forward, out of control.

There was no way she could fool herself into thinking Josh had lured her into his web. The seduction had been all her doing.

How could she look Josh in the eye tomorrow morning and explain her behavior? She fingered her swollen lips and opened her eyes.

And how could she keep it from happening again?

Josh was drinking coffee and reading the morning paper at the kitchen table when Taylor braved her way into the room. Groggy from a fitful night's sleep, she poured herself a mug, fortified herself with a long swallow, then took a seat next to him.

Josh set the paper down and stared at her, his face not giving her a clue as to how he felt about what had happened. He waited for her to speak first, which was very unnerving, and she almost forgot what she'd rehearsed half of the night.

"About yesterday…" she eyed him, waiting for some sort of reaction. Nothing. "I wish I could explain why I think…it happened." There was no way she would tell him, or anyone, about her mother and Max or the journals. "But…well, can we skip the postmortem and talk about where we go from here?"

He motioned toward her with his palm up and nodded curtly. "You have the floor." He wasn't making this any easier. But would *she* if the situation were reversed?

She thought about telling him that she'd decided to move back to the ranch, but she lost her nerve. Besides, she should discuss it with Max first, see what he thought.

Josh was still watching her. She took a deep breath and blurted out the only nonconfrontational thing she could think of. "Can we start over? Slower this time?"

He arched an eyebrow and lowered his head in a way that said, "You're the one who rushed things," but he was kind enough not to say it. Instead he said, "Do I have any choice?"

She twisted the mug in her hands and stared into the dark liquid, feeling guilty for creating such a mess. "I'd like for us to take time to get to know each other—really know each other."

She peered up through her lashes when he didn't speak and was relieved to find a rakish tilt to his head and a mischievous smile.

"And then?"

Her heart pumped harder beneath her pullover.

"And then we'll see."

Eight

After the morning session was over, Taylor reminded Josh that she had another patient at the clinic and that his sisters-in-law wanted to see her today. She handed him some iced tea, said she would be back for the afternoon workout, and then made a beeline for the door, grateful for any reason to put distance between them.

She found Hank outside the barn and he readily agreed to sleep at the house without question, which fit into her new plan nicely. Then she headed for the ranch, wondering what awaited her there. It would be nice to think of something besides Josh for a while, she thought, regardless of what Jenny and Savannah were up to.

But as soon as she stepped into the kitchen, she could see that the cat was out of the bag regarding yesterday's events. Jenny and Savannah stopped talking the second she entered. They looked as if they were biting the insides of their cheeks to keep from cracking up, the gazes that flitted between them speaking volumes.

Taylor helped herself to iced tea with her back to the women, hoping the heat in her cheeks would subside quickly. She should have expected this—that Shane would tell Jenny about his suspicions. And Jenny would surely tell Savannah, since they'd been best friends forever.

A part of her wanted to spin around and tell the pair that what may or may not have gone on between Josh and herself was none of their business. But she knew they meant no harm, that the Malones were a tight family. And if she were honest with herself, she felt flattered that they might be hoping something *was* going on.

She drank her tea, refilled it, and decided she was getting way ahead of herself. It didn't matter what they thought about the match; she wasn't anywhere near ready for such a commitment, and surely Josh wasn't. On a sigh, she turned around, leaned against the counter and eyed the women.

"Shane said you wanted to see me." She kept her voice even, acting as though she hadn't noticed the exchange when she'd walked in. They glanced at each other before answering, a look of disappointment passing between them. Obviously, discussing her love life wasn't on the agenda this morning, and they had wished it was.

Savannah picked up Chris who had been sitting on the floor next to the center cutting board. She hitched him higher on her hip, kissed his chubby little cheek, and waited for Jenny to explain.

Jenny hedged for only a moment. "We were thinking Josh could use something special to look forward to." She paused to look at Savannah and that was their undoing. When a snort sounded at the back of Savannah's throat, Jenny laughed aloud. She tried to speak, but lost it again. Finally, she said, "Sorry. We really aren't laughing *at* you, you know? We've both been there—"

"Done that!" Savannah added between giggles.

Jenny pulled herself together. "It must be in the genes. Malone men are simply irresistible."

Taylor couldn't help but chuckle. They were trying to make her one of them, and the idea felt surprisingly good. She hoped they wouldn't be too disappointed if nothing developed between her and Josh.

Would *she?*

She sucked on an ice cube, remembering she was here to escape such thoughts—at least for a while.

"Okay," Jenny said. "We won't stick our noses in—"

"For now," Savannah said, interrupting with a wink.

"What we were trying to tell you—before we got side-tracked—was that we want to throw a party."

Savannah set the baby down and leaned her elbows against the counter. "We were thinking the Fourth of July. Josh never had a housewarming or anything when he moved out there. The Fourth would give us another excuse."

"We'd do all the cooking," Jenny said. "And the guys could take care of the liquid refreshments and some fireworks. What do you think?"

The Fourth was only a couple of weeks away. Would she and Josh be friends, enemies...or lovers by then?

Damn! She had to stop obsessing over this man.

Savannah stepped from behind the counter. "Do you think it's too soon? Too much for him now?"

Taylor abandoned her personal concerns and shared a smile with the excited pair in front of her. "Sounds like a great idea." She watched them visibly slump with relief. "What do you want me to do?"

Savannah and Jenny looked at each other and shrugged. Then Savannah spoke up. "Maybe you could get Josh to write out a list of people he'd like to invite."

Taylor wondered if Josh would take to the idea of a party at all. And if so, was she the right one to broach the subject?

Jenny reached for the pitcher of iced tea and poured herself a glass. "We can ask him if you prefer."

"No," Taylor said, rinsing her glass in the sink and putting it into the dishwasher. "I'll handle it. And let me know what else I can do to help, okay?" She turned around and noticed that they both seemed pleased with themselves, as if stage one of their conspiracy had worked.

As before, she pretended not to notice. Instead she asked, "Is Max with a patient?"

The baby started to fuss and Savannah picked him up again. "I don't think so. Last I saw him, he was catching up on his reading in the office."

"Thanks. I need to talk to him." She left the kitchen as the pair comforted little Chris. Behind her she heard Jenny saying she couldn't wait for her turn at motherhood.

Taylor slowed her pace to Max's office feeling a sudden emptiness. Home, husband, children. They had it all—everything Taylor wanted someday. She pictured the adorable faces of Billy and the baby and wondered how many years it would take before she could afford to have a child of her own. She'd hardly put a dent in her student loans and she didn't want someone else raising her children. One good thing—once her finances were in order, she had skills that could be used part-time. Right here at the ranch. Or the farm. She sighed loudly. There she went again. Like a broken record she was back in the same old groove with her premature thoughts.

She turned the corner and spotted Max behind his desk. He rose immediately and crossed to her, extending an arm in the direction of the side chairs. She sat in one and he in the other.

It was difficult to look at Max these days and not imagine him in his prime, how he must have appeared when he worked with Mom. Even now he posed a striking figure. His grooming impeccable, the gray at his temples giving him a wise and distinguished look. She wondered if he ever knew the depths of her mother's feelings for him.

"To what do I owe this pleasure?" His easy smile turned quickly downward when she didn't answer immediately. "There isn't something wrong with Josh, is there?"

She shook her head. "No, not at all. He's frustrated at the lack of progress, but we've both seen that before."

Max nodded, folding his arms and stroking his chin pensively. "Do you think he's trying too hard? I mean…could we be doing other things to take his mind off his legs, help him relax a little?"

Taylor had to look away and hope her face didn't reflect her thoughts. Surely he hadn't heard about yesterday, too, had he? No. If he had, it would be the last thing he would allude to now.

Max shifted in his chair and faced her. "I forgot to tell you, but I talked to the manufacturer Josh ordered the new plane from. They're looking into special hand controls. As much as I was opposed to his flying, I know how much he loves it. What do you think?"

She thought about it a moment, then slowly nodded her head. "In the sky, as a pilot, he may feel equal to any man—with or without the use of his legs." She nodded again, more enthusiastically. "It's a great idea." And it would get him outside of the house, something she'd been unsuccessful in doing so far. Even after his brothers had built the ramp at the side door, Josh had hidden his handicap behind closed doors, only letting Hank and the family see him in the chair.

"I think we should wait till we're sure it can be done properly before we tell Josh. Wouldn't want to get his hopes up."

"I agree," she said.

Max slapped his knees and started to rise. "Good, then—"

Taylor held his arm and he dropped back down. "There's something else." She took a deep breath and got right to the point. "I'd like to move my things back to the ranch." Max opened his mouth to argue, but she plunged forward. "I've spoken with Hank and he'll spend nights as long as necessary. I'll still do the workouts with him, but I'd like to stay here at night." She could see the questions creasing his brow, so she opted for a lame excuse. "I—I miss the girls...our time in the kitchen together...the children." He didn't look too convinced. "Besides, maybe it would be better if he had a little time alone...to learn to fend for himself. It might even help his self-esteem if he knew he could manage without me constantly there."

Max studied her face, his head cocked to one side. Finally he stood. "If Hank's willing and you think it might help, I trust your judgment." He paused a moment, then added. "I'll go find Shane and Ryder...talk to them about moving your things back here when they're done for the day."

"Thanks, Max."

He patted her shoulder and left the room.

She *was* doing the right thing, wasn't she?

She pushed out of her chair. Of course she was. All she had to do now was convince Josh. She rounded the corner to the clinic, picked up the chart for the patient waiting in the next room, then paused to give Josh one final thought. If she presented the news just the right way, maybe he would see that her moving back here was best for both of them.

Taylor spotted Josh sitting in front of the window, and she sprinted up the ramp and opened the kitchen door. She smiled at him and asked, "Is there any of that roast beef left?"

"All of it," he said, looking a little suspicious of her breezy manner.

"How about if I make us a couple sandwiches. I'm starved." She opened the refrigerator and pulled out the ingredients.

"Okay." Which sounded more like, What are you up to now?

She took their plates and tea to the table where Josh was drumming his fingers, his gaze fixed on her face. She sat across from him and bowed her head a moment, having much more on her mind than blessing the food they were about to eat. *Please, Lord, give me wisdom to make the right decisions—for Josh and for me.* She looked up and Josh was still eyeing her, waiting for her to fill him in.

"So what are Savannah and Jenny up to? What are they scheming this time?" he asked.

Taylor thought they were scheming more than a party, but she decided to give him the abbreviated version. "They want to have a Fourth of July party—food, drink, fireworks, invite friends...the whole nine yards." She could already see the doubts behind his eyes and feared his reaction to the next piece of news. "And they want to hold it here...sort of a housewarming."

Josh stopped eating and put his sandwich back on his plate, his gaze fixed on the crust.

"It's still a couple of weeks away, Josh. A lot could happen between now and then. You could be on crutches...or a cane."

"And if nothing changes?"

"Either way, it's time you came out of hiding, don't you think?"

"Because I might always be in this chair. That's what you really mean, don't you? It's time to prepare for the worst."

In part, yes. But he'd never hear that from her. "Actually, I was thinking that if you start taking your mind off yourself and resume some semblance of your old life, maybe feeling will return to your legs quicker. You know—like infertile couples who file for adoption and find themselves pregnant soon after. It's strange what the mind can do."

"And you think a party is going to help?"

"It's only one thing."

He peered at her from the side of his face. "What else did you have in mind?"

"Going for a ride...up into the mountains, looking for wildlife, smelling the sage and the flowers, feeling the sunshine." She smiled at the happy thought. When was the last time *she* stopped to smell the roses?

"Exactly when are we supposed to do this?"

"As soon as you finish everything on your plate."

At last he flashed her one of his mischievous smiles. "If I finish every crumb, do I get dessert, too?"

She caught the twinkle in his eye. "You have a one-track mind, Joshua Malone." She smiled back, feeling warmer than the day called for.

"Maybe I do. But you can't fool me anymore, Ms. Phillips. I've seen a glimpse—"

Taylor popped out of her chair and went to the sink. "Eat up. The day's wasting." If she thought about their time on the mat once more, she thought she might scream. Or…

"Okay, I'll be a good boy and eat my lunch…and then we'll go for a ride. But I want you to know I didn't agree to any party."

She exhaled and took pleasure in the small victory. Later she would push for the party. And later yet she would tell him she was moving back to the ranch. That would be the tough one, but there was no point spoiling the afternoon by saying something now.

She'd already repacked her things in their original boxes early this morning, and they were waiting by the bedroom door. Knowing Josh, he wasn't going to take too kindly to her decision. But then again, maybe she could make him understand her motives. If they wanted to take things slowly, living under the same roof would only complicate matters.

She just needed to relax and the right words would come.

Hank had seen them coming down the ramp, and he helped Josh up into the front seat of Taylor's old Ford. He also agreed to keep an eye out for them when they returned from their excursion. He handed Josh the pair of binoculars he'd requested then raised his arm over his head for a hearty wave before heading back to the barn.

Taylor backed out and Josh called from the window, "Thanks, Hank."

"I miss it more than I thought," Josh said after a moment. "I liked checking on the animals in the barn...and riding the combine, the smell of fresh-cut wheat and hay, milking a cow or two. And most of all watching things grow...and being outside, no matter the weather."

"You can have it all again, Josh."

"Can I?" He gazed to the side and expelled a long sigh out the open window.

"Yep. One bite at a time. Starting right now. Where shall we go?"

"There's a two-track that leads around the western side of the MoJoes, winds up quite a ways. It's just past that last irrigation arm." He pointed down the road and sat back, gazing out over his acres of wheat fields, a brief sadness stealing a moment or two. He'd missed most of his first season. And still he couldn't walk. He wished they were in his pickup, with him behind the wheel. But he knew that wasn't possible and that this lower seat was necessary, just as he understood all the other changes in his life. Yet that didn't make him like it any better.

When Taylor passed the fields and turned up the path, he balled his fists into the seat and forced his body taller, adjusting his view as well as his attitude. It was a truly gorgeous summer day, the first that he had witnessed close-up in ages. He wasn't going to waste it.

"You sure this old thing is going to make it up this steep, bumpy road?"

"This is the worse part. Gets better up ahead. Try putting it in Low."

She did and they chugged higher up the path until finally the ground leveled and they crept to a stop near one of his favorite precipices. The valley in front of them was deep and wide, alive with colors he wished he could paint.

"Oh, Josh. This is so...*beautiful* doesn't describe it."

He loved this spot, and now the look on her face said

she did, too. They sat side by side and simply stared out the dusty windshield. He was about to reach for her hand when she put the car in reverse.

"Leaving already?" he asked.

She smiled over at him. "Fat chance, cowboy." She parked parallel to the view and cut the engine.

"Now you can't see as well," he said.

She rolled her eyes and continued to smile. "A little patience...please!" She got out of the car, came around to his side and opened his door. "I have a blanket in the trunk."

He sized up the situation. Helping him down onto the ground next to the car wouldn't be so bad, but getting him back in might be tricky. As strong as Taylor was, he hated putting so much weight on her.

"I have a few walkers in here, too," she called from the back of the car.

"A few?"

"I collect them...from families who don't need them anymore. Always someone who does."

There was so much he didn't know about this woman, though her generosity of spirit shouldn't have surprised him. He turned his head and watched her bring a blanket and walker alongside. His pride had kept him from even trying to use one of those contraptions before, but supporting his weight on something other than Taylor seemed the logical solution. He sighed heavily and acted as though it were a big deal, when in fact he was pleased with her foresight. "Okay, let's give it a try."

Taylor spread the blanket on the ground next to the car and then positioned the walker just so. With a hefty grunt, Josh pulled his weight over the walker. Together they maneuvered so that she could take his weight as he slid his back down the side of the car. Beads of sweat ran from their temples as they exhaled in unison after the taxing ordeal.

"Is it time for a nap, yet?" he asked, short of breath.

Taylor laughed, leaned her head against the car and closed her eyes. Josh watched her tilt her face to the sun, a smile lingering on lips he remembered too well, lips he wished he could touch with his own this very moment.

She opened her eyes and gazed at him. After an inventory of his face, she asked, "So does this mean we're starting again?"

He smiled and nodded. "Thanks for dragging me out here...literally."

"I'd like to say 'no sweat' but as you can see—" She lowered her forehead and blotted it with the hem of her knit top. It was sky blue, much like her eyes. And formfitting—something else to remind him...

She caught the direction of his gaze. "So you think we could work on a friendship first...please?"

"If we must."

She eyed him from the side of her face, seeming more amused than angry. "Slowly?"

"How slowly?"

With her head she pointed to the view beyond and ignored his question.

Nine

They scanned the serene vista in companionable silence, and Taylor felt a sense of peace and contentment she hadn't felt since...since she couldn't remember when. This day was meant to be for Josh, but it was working wonders for her. Between her mother's death and Josh's accident, she hadn't realized just how tense and hectic her life had become. If they sat here all afternoon and didn't utter a word she would be happy.

But eventually Josh asked, "Ever been to downtown Joeville?"

She shook her head.

"Malone property stops at the ridge. Beyond that is the actual town—what there is of it. The township owns it."

She squinted her eyes. "Exactly where is it?"

"I left the binoculars on the seat." Taylor jumped up and got them and he pointed to the east. She lifted the lenses to her face. "See the small white steeple in the gap between the tallest trees? A little more to the left."

She turned and adjusted the focus. "I think I see it. Is there only one church?"

"Yep. That's Joeville Community Church. Hannah talks about it a lot...and of course, Billy. That's where he goes to Bible school on Sundays. The rest of us go when we can. See anything else?"

"A few shorter buildings. Can't see much with all the trees."

"There isn't much to see. A general store with the post office attached. Then there's Hadley's Hardware and Feed, a gas station, not much else. About sixty people short of being a ghost town, but they're a hardy bunch. Mostly older folk now with a few young women still living at home."

"No young men?"

He folded his arms and flashed her a cocky white smile. "Nope."

"What's so amusing?"

"Guess that makes me the last bachelor in Joeville." He wiggled his eyebrows up and down, and she laughed.

"And damn proud of it, right?" She swatted his shoulder with the back of her hand. "I think it's time for you to get back to the farm and work off some of that excess energy."

With some doing, they were back in the car and winding down the dusty path. Taylor was enjoying the miles of wildflowers and nearly missed a scrawny coyote crossing in front of them. She braked hard and Josh jerked against his seat belt.

"Sorry. You okay?"

He didn't seem the least bit disturbed. Instead he reached across the seat and laid his hand on her thigh. "I'm fine. More than fine." His gaze lingered on hers, then he looked straight ahead and said, "Thank you for today."

Such simple words, yet they created a tingling sensation, a scary and delicious feeling all at the same time. "You're welcome," she said, and drove on toward the farm.

As they turned up the drive she saw Shane's Explorer by the side door and Ryder carrying a box. Her heart raced and she mentally thumped her forehead. How could she have forgotten to tell Josh about her decision to move back to the ranch? She'd meant to say something when—

"Taylor?" He eyed her suspiciously, the relaxed warmth she'd seen on his face seconds earlier completely vanished.

"I—I planned to tell you. I just didn't expect them here so soon." She cut the engine several yards from the Explorer and faced Josh. "I'm sorry we didn't talk about this earlier, but I decided to move back to the ranch. It's better I don't stay here. Trust me."

"Trust you?" His laugh was caustic. She watched his jaw muscles grinding and she could hardly blame him for being angry.

"This doesn't change anything. I'll still come over. On the days I don't have other patients, we'll have time between morning and afternoon workouts to visit or go for a ride. It's just that things will be less complicated if I'm not here all the time."

The fury in his eyes seemed barely contained. "Who is it you don't trust, Taylor? Me or you?"

His question caught her off guard. "I—I don't know."

"Don't you?" If he could have jumped out of the car and slammed the door behind him, she knew he would. The fact that he couldn't only served to make matters worse. He flung open his door and used his arms to swivel slowly in his seat.

Taylor saw Shane approaching and got out to meet him halfway, knowing if she stayed with Josh another minute they both might say things they would regret. Besides, she was starting to second-guess her decision.

Shane stopped and she whispered, "He's pretty upset, so beware. I'll get his chair out of the trunk."

Shane nodded and strode to Josh's side of the car. Taylor brought the chair around and Josh shot her a look of loathing. "I don't need your help. You want to go back to the ranch so bad, then go."

"But your afternoon therapy—"

"Just go!" he shouted, his expression hurting her more than his words.

Shane helped Josh out of the car and spoke softly to Taylor. "I'll help him today. Why don't I use your car and you can head back with Ryder and your things?" His eyes weren't asking; they were saying, Please go. Now.

She glanced at Josh, but he refused to look her way. Moisture formed on the top of her lashes and a knot pushed at the back of throat. This hadn't gone at all as she'd planned...and it was all her fault. She turned and walked toward Ryder, her head down, her emotions careening between hurt and embarrassment, frustration and...and what?

Too emotional to analyze anything, she stepped into the Explorer and rode back to the ranch, grateful that Ryder didn't say a word.

"A little hard on her, wouldn't you say?" Shane asked, as he and Josh watched the cloud of dust behind the departing Explorer.

Josh threw him a derisive look and didn't respond.

"She's been busting her butt to help you."

"Yeah, I know," he said with an attitude. "Help a gimp, save the world."

"Feeling a little sorry for ourselves, are we?"

Josh snapped back. "What's this *we* business? Don't see you sitting in this chair." With all the strength he could muster, Josh spun the wheels in the gravel drive and made his way to the ramp at the side door. Beads of sweat dripped into his eyes from the effort, and he paused to rub them dry and catch his breath.

Shane pushed him up the long incline and this time Josh didn't refuse the help. Once inside, Shane retrieved a couple of cans of beer from the refrigerator and held one out to Josh. He took it, feeling like a jerk and giving Shane his most contrite look. Shane turned a chair around and straddled it backward. He sipped his beer and seemed in no hurry.

Eventually, Josh slumped in his chair, the fight seeping out of him. "Guess I handled that well, huh?"

Shane swiped at the moisture on the can.

"About that crack a minute ago—"

"Forget it." Shane lifted his can and drank.

Josh shook his head and released a long sigh. "Look, Shane...if it weren't for you, I'd be toast. You had nothing to do with the rest. When are you going to stop beating yourself up over this?"

Shane finished his beer and set it down with a clang. "When you're out of that chair and back to normal."

Taylor dried pots and pans and helped the women clean up after supper. There was talk of the forthcoming party and the food and countless other details, but during it all Taylor was aware of their questioning glances. They didn't ask, but she could imagine their thoughts.... What happened between you and Josh? Why are you back here?

Most of that night and the next morning, driving to Bozeman, she was asking herself these same questions.

What did she want to happen between herself and Josh? Why was she still holding a part of herself back? Yes, they had had a little incident yesterday, but that was all it was—a little incident. So why had she chosen to stay away from him today rather than return and make amends?

There were patients at the hospital she wanted to check on, ones in the care of her temporary replacement. And surely there was mail at her apartment, maybe phone messages, too.

But in her heart, she knew these were convenient excuses. When Shane had offered to help Josh again today, she'd jumped at the chance without a second thought.

A little time and space might help her get things into perspective, she told herself, pulling into the parking lot next to her apartment. Still, an inner voice told her she was running away. But exactly what was she running from? She climbed the steps feeling as though she'd just returned from a marathon, her legs leaden, her chest tight. Was she afraid of spending a lifetime with a man who couldn't walk? She didn't think that was it. She checked with her internal muse. No. That wasn't it. Besides, she hadn't given up hope that that would change someday soon.

She turned the key in the door and stepped into her old apartment, a wave of musty heat swirling around her. As she pulled up blinds and opened windows, she kept searching for answers.

Was she afraid she might be acting out her mother's unfulfilled fantasies of Max instead of having true feelings for Josh? On this point she wasn't sure. She didn't think so, yet something unsettling kept nagging her about Mom and the Malones.

Weary of all the questions, she dropped into the swivel chair beside her rolltop desk and noticed the light flashing on the answering machine. She pushed the Playback button and listened to the tape whirl backward. Pencil in hand, she started making notes of those who had called. Then she heard the familiar voice of her father, and she put the pencil down and smiled.

"We miss you, sweetheart. Michael and I were thinking of coming out for the long holiday weekend...if that's okay with you. Give me a call. Love you."

She punched the speed-dial number on her phone, and Michael picked it up on the second ring. She had expected a recording and was pleasantly surprised to hear his voice. "What are you doing home?" she asked. "Thought you'd be pounding nails somewhere."

"And hello to you, too, sis. Just caught me grabbing some lunch. Was half out the door." He laughed easily and she could picture his smiling gray eyes and brown ponytail—a hairstyle that had caused more than one discussion between father and son. "So can we come? Is it an okay time for you?"

Even if it weren't, she couldn't say no after hearing his voice and feeling her own excitement. "I'd love to have you. But can you get enough time off? It's a long way, even if you take turns and drive straight through.''

"That's what's so cool—besides seeing you. One of Dad's customers gave us two frequent flyer tickets that were about to expire. Free plane tickets! Do you believe it?''

This would be Michael's first flight and his first trip to Montana. A bubble of happiness formed at the back of her throat, and she felt as though she might cry from pure joy. She couldn't wait to show Michael the mountains, the animals, the Big Sky.

"You still there, sis?''

"Book those seats, kid, and let me know when you'll be arriving.''

She gave him her number at the ranch and explained the temporary arrangement before they talked briefly about their father. He had his moments, Michael said, but work had kept him from giving in to the grief. Soon they said their goodbyes and she clung to the dead phone in her hand, anticipation of the visit giving her a high she hadn't felt since...since...

She'd made love with Josh.

She heaved a sigh. Everything came back to Josh. Nothing, not even her dad's and Michael's visit, could distract her from thinking of that man.

She hiked back down the stairs to the bank of mailboxes and emptied the crammed cubicle. Halfway up the steps she came to a dead stop.

Oh, no. Fourth of July weekend. Josh's party.

She started up again with an uncomfortable cramping in her midsection. Josh wouldn't mind their coming... assuming he was speaking to her by then. In fact, he would probably love to meet them and be very hospitable, as would all the Malones.

She closed the door behind her and flopped onto the sofa, stretching out on her back, hands behind her head, eyes closed.

But Dad and Max in the same room.

Had this ever happened before? Had they ever met? Obviously Max knew about Dad, but had Dad ever found out how Mom felt about Max?

She thought of the journals and wished they were still in the attic, that she didn't know her mother's secrets. It was almost as though her mother had wanted her to know. But why? The questions wouldn't cease. Dad, Max, Mom, Josh. Nothing made sense, yet everything screamed a warning of some sort that was impossible to ignore. Would her dad and Max have an ugly encounter at the party? Was that what she feared?

She clasped her hands to her ears and growled aloud, thrusting herself off the sofa and into action. Work. That's what she needed right now. Nothing could be solved lying around all day. She started ticking off a list in her head—first she would visit a few patients, then come back here, pay some bills, change the message on the machine and shut the windows. And if she timed it right, she would get back to the ranch at bedtime, too exhausted to think about the Malones or her family or whatever else was grating deep within her subconscious.

Thursday morning Taylor drove toward the farm feeling every bit as anxious as when she'd left nearly forty-eight hours before. Not only did she have to apologize for creating the problem Tuesday, but now Max had asked her to deliver some news—news that could potentially spell more conflict.

The new plane would arrive today. She hadn't a clue how Josh would react. And if that wasn't enough, she needed to talk to him about Dad and Michael and the party, which most likely wouldn't be an issue with him, but was of growing concern to her.

She pulled up the long drive and took a few steadying breaths. Hank walked out the side door and down the ramp as she stepped from her car.

"Good morning, Hank."

He touched the rim of his hat. "Mornin'."

"How's he doing?" She wanted to ask, What mood is he in? but she didn't feel comfortable putting Hank on the spot.

"Oh, fair to middlin', I'd guess. Better'n most in the same boat." He seemed eager to get going.

"Thanks for all your help, Hank."

He turned and waved over his shoulder. "No problem."

She stared at the door and stalled as long as she could, then she trudged up the ramp, knocked once and let herself in.

It was 8:00 a.m. and Josh was sitting at the kitchen table with a mug of coffee. He wore a white, ribbed T-shirt that stretched taut across his well-developed chest and upper arms, and Taylor's breath hitched in her throat. This wasn't going to be easy—not just discussing things with him, but working with him, touching him...and feeling so out of control.

He was studying her face and didn't say a word. She poured herself some coffee and sat in the chair next to him.

"Josh...I'm really sorry about the way things turned out Tuesday."

His smile was faint, but there was a gentleness around his eyes. "You already told me that when it happened."

"Yes, but—"

"But I overreacted. I was a jerk."

She'd expected anger, not contrition, and it surprised her. She drank from her mug and eyed him over the rim, trying to rein in her emotions and the strong physical reaction he always evoked in her.

"I'm sorry, too," he continued. "I said some stupid things." He looked away and then back. "Taylor, I do trust you. I know you'd never intentionally keep something important from me...something you knew I'd want or need to know."

Was he making a statement or asking for reassurance?

She wasn't sure so she responded with a vigorous shake of her head. "Yes. You're right. I wouldn't...not with any friend."

One of his eyebrows arched. "So we're friends now?"

At least, flashed through her head involuntarily, but she forced a look of nonchalance. "Of course." She met his gaze and wondered how on this green earth she would be able to take things slowly with this man she longed to touch, whose lips invited her closer, whose—

"Taylor?"

She shook her head. "Hmm?"

"Is there something wrong?"

Her top was sticking to her back and chest. She wanted to blouse it out and give it a few shakes. Instead, she put her coffee down and eyed him again. "There are a few things we need to discuss before we go to work."

He crossed his arms and faked a worried frown. "Oh, oh. Ground rules."

His good-natured ribbing was doing little to relax her. "No. Actually I have two messages to deliver...one from your dad and one from mine. Well, the one from mine isn't exactly a message. That can wait till later." She was tripping over her tongue, finding it hard to concentrate on anything but the blue-gray eyes looking back at her.

"What did Dr. Dad want you to tell me?"

She glanced at his teasing lips, then blurted out the message before she could forget it. "Your new plane is being delivered today." She watched a shadow pass over his face and wondered if he was remembering the accident.

He unfolded his arms and shoved his hands beneath his legs, his gaze somewhere remote. "When I ordered it, I was so excited about getting a new one." He leaned forward. "It has a GPS—Global Positioning System—that can pinpoint any place on earth within three feet. Before GPS, dusters had to use a ground crew to physically mark rows and..."

Josh fell silent and his expression was one of defeat

when he focused on Taylor's face. "I'm never going to walk again, am I?"

She stared into his eyes and her heart ached. "I don't know, Josh."

A cynical smile lifted a corner of his mouth. "I guess we really are friends. I was expecting you to say 'Sure you are. Don't give up hope.'"

"I don't want you to give up hope." She leaned closer, wanting desperately to take his hand, but afraid of her own emotions. "I didn't say you won't walk again, Josh. I just said I don't know."

His face softened. "Fair enough." He sighed loudly. "But still…a new plane is useless to me. A pilot needs working feet for the rudder pedals."

"Unless that pilot has a loving and knowledgeable father who had hand controls installed." In a flash she saw a flicker of excitement in his eyes, the wheels turning with the possibilities.

"Probably couldn't do a chandelle," he said, as if thinking aloud. "No, too sharp a turn without feet. But I could manage a teardrop." He nodded his head slowly. "It's not as fast or efficient, but it would get the job done."

Taylor smiled, glad she was the bearer of good news, after all. "And when the feeling in your legs returns, you can have the controls removed."

"*When?*" he asked. "Don't you mean *if?*"

"I'm still optimistic, aren't you?"

Now she saw that familiar rakish look back on his face. "Even if I wasn't, I'm not crazy enough to stop therapy. What red-blooded man wouldn't want to spend hours up close and personal with such a—"

She shot him a warning look.

"Good friend?"

Taylor laughed. "Speaking of therapy." She slapped her thighs and stood.

"Yeah, yeah." He unlocked his chair and spun away

from the table. "But what about *your* dad? Didn't you say you had a message from him, too?"

"First things first. It can keep till lunch."

"Slave driver. When does a guy get to have some fun around here?"

"When his new plane arrives and he takes me for a ride."

He shot her a devilish smile over his shoulder, and she wondered what she had gotten herself into now.

Ten

The temperature climbed into the mid-eighties, and the small oscillating fan on the kitchen counter churned the hot air. Occasionally a gentle breeze wafted through the open windows, providing some relief.

The morning session had been one of the hardest for both Josh and Taylor, each determined to make a difference, each hoping today would be the day that feeling would return to his legs.

It hadn't happened this morning, but Josh felt an unexplainable optimism in the thick air. At times like this, he thought anything was possible...as long as he had Taylor in his life.

He watched her at the kitchen window as he drank lemonade and waited for the plane to arrive. The simple grace of her caught his breath. The serene smile on her face was more beautiful than the scenery she seemed to be enjoying.

"It's something else, isn't it?" he said softly.

"It sure is." Her gaze didn't stray from the mountains

and wilderness that surrounded them, and her voice was barely a whisper when she spoke again.

"I can't remember how old I was when I decided I'd go to school in Montana. I'd listen to Mom's stories and imagine what it would be like." She tipped her head back and blinked. Then she pulled out a chair next to Josh at the table and sat down, her smile more fragile now.

"It's so much grander than I ever dreamed." She topped off both their glasses with the pitcher on the table. "Michigan was the home of my youth…a good one, a safe one. But I knew once I moved out here that I would never return…not to live. I think Montana has been the home of my soul since the day I was born." She wrinkled her nose in an endearing way. "Sounds silly, doesn't it?"

She met his gaze and he shook his head, unable to swallow for the longest time. Photos not yet taken flashed in his mind's eye. Family photos, here at the farm, surrounded by children and laughter, Christmases and toys.

And Taylor looking up at him adoringly.

Taylor touched his hand with hers and he flinched. "Josh? What's wrong?"

He shook his head again, wishing he could share the moment with her, but not wanting to spook her. "Just thinking how much I love this place, that's all."

She glanced around the kitchen, her gaze lingering on the cross-paned glass cupboard doors and then the black cast-iron wood stove angled in the corner near them. "I keep meaning to ask you…who did all this? I mean the refurbishing." She tilted her head and scanned the coved ceiling. "It looks like it was built yesterday, but this place has to be over—"

"Over a hundred years old," he said, interrupting her and relishing her appreciation of one of his favorite topics. "My great-granddad built it and lived here till he and his wife died. Grandpa built the original ranch where Dad was born. Later Dad added the clinic and extra wings so all of us could have our own space under one roof."

"I bet he wasn't too pleased when you moved here to the farm."

"You could say that. But he's gotten used to it." He smiled and cocked his head toward Taylor. "He roars like a lion, but you've probably noticed there's a soft, furry kitten under that facade."

Instead of laughing or agreeing with him, as Josh thought she would, she averted her gaze and seemed a million miles away. He wondered what he'd said that had caused her to drift off. But just as suddenly she was back, sipping her lemonade, her eyes smiling and peering over the rim.

"You didn't answer my question. Who did all this?" she asked.

Josh tried not to puff out his chest when he answered. "I did. Took about three years in my spare time. Shane and Ryder helped when they could. Mostly I worked by myself." She seemed genuinely impressed, which was exactly what he'd set out to do.

"But you had a carpenter help you, right?"

"Nope. Bought some books and taught myself." Now he did puff out his chest, wishing he had a couple of suspenders to snap for emphasis. "Can't say I didn't make mistakes…a lot of them. Had to tear out almost as much as I put in. But I learned. And I loved every minute of it."

"Obviously." Her gaze stopped roving around the cozy room and settled on him. "I'm truly impressed." She started to say more, then leaned back, a debate reflected on her face. She finished her drink, then expelled a long breath. "I don't think I ever told you, but Dad and Michael are both carpenters."

He wondered why she seemed so uncomfortable all of a sudden.

"They're coming for a visit soon."

"Terrific. You'll have to bring them out. They can critique my work." He laughed and waited for her smile. None came. And still he couldn't see the cause for her concern.

"The only time they can get away is Fourth of July...the long weekend."

"I bet. I hear construction is pretty hot in Michigan right now." Why was she looking so conflicted? "Taylor, what is it?"

"Your party...I want to be here...I've promised to help. But I want to spend time with my family, too."

Josh blew out a breath of relief. "Well, that's easy enough to fix. Bring them to the party! I get to meet them, they get to see the place...and they can meet the rest of the Malones, too. Problem solved."

She stood abruptly and carried her plate and glass to the sink, giving him her back in response. What wasn't she telling him?

"Thanks, Josh. I'll pass the invitation on." She took her time at the sink until finally she chuckled and turned around. "Michael would think he died and went to heaven if he got to ride a horse or saw a moose in the wild." She stared at her shoes. "And Dad...Dad would love this house."

"Well, good. Then it's settled. I know you, Phillips. If you want them to come to the party, they don't have a snowball's chance finagling their way out of it. And you know everyone will make them feel right at home in no time."

She smiled and seemed somewhat mollified. Maybe her mood had something to do with her mom. Though Taylor rarely showed it, he knew she must still be grieving...and probably would be for some time. He was debating whether to broach the subject when he heard a familiar sound from above. The drone of an engine drew closer.

Josh listened, excitement and fear playing a duet behind his ribs. The fear was natural, he assured himself. Like getting back on a horse after a fall. He'd done that often enough. It was only the anticipation of the first time that was giving him the jitters. Once he was in the air, he knew all would be well.

"Ready to go?" he asked Taylor, pretending he didn't notice her somber expression. Whatever the problem, she didn't seem in the mood to discuss it now. "The pilot should be touching down soon," he said, storing his questions for later. The landing strip was over a mile from the house and it would take a while to get them both into the car and on the way.

Taylor carried his empty glass to the sink and he noticed that her hands were shaking. "Are you okay?"

She turned and leaned against the counter, gripping the edge with white knuckles. "Oh, sure. No problem."

"Uh-huh."

"Really!"

"It can't be the flying thing now, can it? You flew with me before...when I took you to the airport."

She rolled her eyes and pushed off the counter, looking more playful than before. "I know. That's what I'm remembering."

He laughed and wheeled toward the door. "Don't worry. No hotdogging today." From the screen door he called back to her. "There's a black leather flight bag in the bedroom closet. Mind getting it for me?"

He listened to her rummaging around in the next room and imagined the two of them landing the plane somewhere private, hopping down to the ground and running with her through the fields, splashing water on her from a cold spring.

Someday.

But today he would do his best to enjoy what he had: a new plane and a new friend.

He chuckled out loud at the word *friend*. Had he ever had a female friend who wasn't more? But then Taylor *had* been more. And in his heart he hoped she would be again.

She returned with the flight bag, grabbed the handles of his chair and guided him down the ramp, across the gravel and to her car.

The pilot was walking around the new Cessna when they

pulled up alongside. He removed his cap, wiped his brow with the back of his wrist and then stepped forward to greet them.

"I'm Gary Cullen. You must be Joshua Malone." He stretched out his tanned arm and gripped Josh's hand for a quick shake.

Josh nodded to his side. "This is…my friend…Taylor Phillips. She's going along with us. I assume we're flying you back."

Gary laughed. "It's a long walk if you don't." He looked from the chair to the plane and rubbed the side of his neck. "You going to be able to get out when you get back here?"

"There's lots of help around here." He glanced at Taylor. "Besides, you wouldn't believe how strong this lady is."

"Oh-h-kay," Gary said, not sounding too convinced. "Then let's get this show on the road."

Gary explained all the new gadgets and hand controls, and Taylor watched from the bench seat in the back as Josh got the feel of things long before they dropped Gary at the airport in Bozeman.

Gary stood at the bottom of the steps and shouted over the engine noise. "Call me anytime if you have a question or a problem."

"Will do." Josh gave a mock salute and added, "Thanks for everything."

Gary waved and started walking across the tarmac. Taylor crawled into the copilot's seat, and Josh taxied away from the terminal, waiting for the tower to give him clearance for takeoff.

As soon as they were in the air again, Taylor watched the joy on Josh's face. And again the day on the mat flashed in her memory and she could feel the heat on her own face. More and more lately, she found herself daydreaming about his lips and the warmth of his breath on her neck. And with certainty she knew it would happen again. It was just a matter of time.

Josh banked the plane and pointed. "See that lookout tower over there?"

"Uh-huh."

"Owned by the U.S. Forest Service. In the old days it was used to spot fires, but planes have taken over those duties now. Ryder and I climbed up it once." He shot her a quick glance. "You have to see the view from up there sometime. Three hundred and sixty degrees of awesome."

She looked at the tall stilts it sat on and noticed a ladder, which she guessed to be almost twenty feet high. "Is there an elevator?"

"Nope." He circled the tower one more time and then headed east for home. "When I can climb those steps, we're coming back." He looked over at her. "Okay?"

"It's a date."

"There's one other little detail I forgot to tell you."

"Which is?"

"It's rented out by the night...so we could sleep over and watch the sunrise if we wanted." She slanted him a look and he added quickly. "Strictly platonic, of course."

She smiled, hiding her true feelings the best she could. "Of course."

Hank was waiting when they got back to the airstrip, and the difficult move of Josh from plane to car was made at a snail's pace under the hot afternoon's sun. Back at the farm, as soon as the car rolled to a stop and Josh was safely seated in his chair, Hank took off like a shot for chores he obviously enjoyed far more than idle conversation.

Once up the ramp and into the kitchen, Josh faced Taylor. "Will you stay for dinner?" He tried his best to say please with his eyes. He wasn't in the mood for a night alone. Usually he enjoyed his solitude, but tonight he longed to talk with Taylor.

About anything. About everything.

The day had been more than simply pleasant. For the most part, except the short time before the plane arrived, things had felt relaxed between them, intimate at times, even when they didn't speak but simply enjoyed the snow-crested mountains, waterfalls and wildlife that teemed below them, all conspiring to give them a glimpse at God's handiwork. And maybe, he thought, to bring them closer together.

Taylor's back was to him and he could feel her indecision.

"You don't have to cook," he said after a while. "We could raid the fridge…or maybe roast hot dogs and marshmallows in front of the hearth. It's supposed to get down into the low fifties tonight. Great night for a fire."

She turned slowly and studied him, as if trying to determine his motives. Or maybe her self-control. Then she walked to the phone on the counter. "Let me call the ranch and be sure there aren't any unexpected patients coming. Sometimes Savannah schedules a patient in the early evening when she knows I'll be there."

The call was quick, and Taylor's face was unrevealing. Either she couldn't stay or she didn't want to. He wasn't sure which. But then she asked, "Do you really have marshmallows?" and he laughed out loud.

"And graham crackers and chocolate, too."

"Just like camp," she said, her warm smile suggesting something more than he dared to dream.

"Great. Then it's settled?"

"But we have work to do in the meantime."

Josh groaned. He had hoped the afternoon excursion would get him out of more therapy today. He should have known better.

When he didn't move fast enough, Taylor grabbed the handles of his chair and pushed him toward the bars. "Think of it this way. This workout will make you one step closer to recovery."

For now, at least, he would like to be one kiss closer to the mat.

After the workout, while Josh rested in his room, Taylor went upstairs and eyed the nightstand. It was probably no accident that she'd left the journals behind. It was becoming more and more difficult to read the words, even though she had questions she wanted answered. But would she like what she found?

Anxiety pressed against her chest until finally she yanked open the drawer and extracted the first journal. The questions weren't going away. There was no point pretending they would.

Toe to heel, she pushed off her shoes, fluffed a couple of pillows against the headboard and read as quickly as she could, flying over the words, resisting the temptation to linger or become too involved, simply looking for answers. And as she turned the last page and read to the end, she expelled a breath she hadn't realized she'd been holding.

Mom and Max had *not* been intimate.

Max had left Ann Arbor for good and Mom had never discussed her feelings for Max with Dad.

Taylor closed her eyes and pressed the book to her chest. She knew she was being selfish in the relief she felt. Mom and Max must have suffered terribly at the time, as well as Dad who must have sensed something was wrong, even if he didn't know exactly what.

Yet their sacrifices meant her freedom. No longer did she have to worry about Dad and Max and the Fourth of July party…or any of the other scenarios that had cluttered her mind and troubled her heart.

She sat up slowly and stretched. The bedside clock read six forty-five. She and Josh had a date at seven. She smiled. *A date.* That's what he'd called it…and she'd liked the sound of it.

She opened the drawer to tuck the journal away and the second one caught her eye. A part of her said, Leave it alone; it can wait. But waiting would only stir those old anxieties again. With great apprehension, she picked it up and sat on the edge of the bed fingering the calico cover.

Please, she prayed, *don't let this one change anything.*

She opened it slowly and saw the date at the top. Nearly four years had passed since the end of the first journal. Already she felt better. She skimmed the first few pages and could see that the subject was her mother's accident, the one that had nearly killed her, that had cost her a kidney. Her thoughts had been about appreciating life, spiritual growth, those kinds of things.

But nowhere did she mention Max's name.

Taylor saw her name often and, just before she closed the book, she saw her father's name and something about him looking like a chipmunk from the mumps he'd contracted from his equally fat-cheeked daughter. Other than that, all seemed well at the Phillips' household. There seemed no need to read on.

Taylor put the book away, her spirits buoyed, new hope for her and Josh bubbling to the surface. All these weeks she had worried over nothing.

She'd showered earlier, so now she stood in the middle of the room in her underwear, wishing she had something different to wear tonight. Josh had seen her in jeans, her old white hospital jacket or sweats—always therapist utilitarian and, well, not too feminine. Then she remembered the few things hanging in the closet that she'd forgotten to repack.

She found a light blue sundress, held it over her in front of the oval free-standing mirror and decided this was the one. Not too tight, not cut too low. Just light and breezy, nothing that said "Come hither" or sent off the wrong message.

After spreading it across the bed, she raced to the bathroom to touch up her hair and apply a little makeup that she kept in her purse. With each stroke of the mascara wand, thoughts of the journals slipped further into the background, a new sense of freedom emerging. At last she could say—and believe—that whatever she felt for Josh had nothing to do with Max and her mother. It was time she accepted that fact, stopped worrying and moved on. And tonight was the perfect time and place to begin anew.

Josh was making paper knots in front of the open hearth when Taylor descended the stairs. He stopped when he spotted her and let out a low whistle of approval. "Who is this lovely creature?"

His smile was infectious and she responded in kind. "Why, it's your date for tonight. Have you forgotten already?" She sauntered over toward him and knelt on one of the overstuffed pillows on the floor next to him.

"Not hardly." His gaze roved the length of her, his smile widening when he returned to her face. "I think I could get used to this date business."

Before she could think twice, she said, "Me, too." The fire hadn't even been built, but already she felt the heat generated between them.

Slow down, she told herself. Enjoy the moment. They had all the time in the world to get to know each other before they...

Well, the rest could wait, she told herself.

He cupped her chin in his hand and smiled down at her tenderly.

Maybe it could wait, she heard a little voice whisper in her head.

But how much longer?

Eleven

Taylor straightened her shoulders and eased away from Josh. "Should I stack a few logs?"

He held up the paper in his lap. "These knots might be more effective if you did."

He chuckled as she turned toward the hearth. She filled the grate with aged wood and could feel him watching her every move. When she turned around he handed her the paper knots, and she found strategic spots under and between the logs. She spotted long matches standing in a tall brass ornament and retrieved one.

Then she paused. Hot dogs over an open fire sounded like fun, but she wasn't sure she could get the first bite down her throat as nervous as she felt. She pivoted and sat cross-legged on a pillow and eyed Josh. "It hasn't cooled off that much yet. Should we wait awhile or are you hungry now?"

"I'm famished, but food can wait."

His eyes sent a suggestive message, but for once she

wasn't offended. How could she be, when she felt the same way? "Should I put on some music?"

He motioned to the rough-sawn cedar shelves behind them. "Whatever you'd like...except opera. I'm not too keen on opera."

"Classical, then?"

"I thought you were from Motown?"

She chuckled. "Ann Arbor is hardly Motown, cowboy."

"Huh!" He raised his chin in a challenging way. "Well, I saw the movie *The Big Chill* and *that* was in Ann Arbor. 'I Heard it Through the Grapevine' sounded pretty Motown to me."

"So what are you saying? You want me to play *The Big Chill?*" He was toying with her in some ritualistic way and she loved every second of it.

He shook his head and eyed her. "No, gorgeous—oh, I meant to tell you, you do look gorgeous in that dress—but *The Big Chill* is as far away from my mind as the moon."

She picked a *Best of Beethoven* CD, inserted it, adjusted the volume to a low setting and then crossed to Josh, taking his hand in hers when he offered it. The simple gesture sent a chill down her bare arms, and she wondered if her will-power could stand the test of his charms another night.

"Why don't I get us something to drink," she said, a little too enthusiastically. She needed to exhale out of his sight. She'd managed to act experienced at this dating business thus far, but this was about as long as she could fake it.

Josh called after her as she left the room. "There's a bottle of wine chilling, if you'd like."

She opened the refrigerator and waved the door a few times, sending much needed cool air in her direction. She was enjoying their playful little banter, but she didn't know how much longer she could keep it up. In truth, her education and career had left little time for such things as dating. There had been a teenage quicky romance, if that's what you called it, but building a relationship was something else.

She found a couple of goblets, grabbed the bottle and took a fortifying breath before returning to Josh.

With filled glasses in hand, Josh said, "To friendship," and clinked his glass to Taylor's. She started to raise the wine to her lips and then he added, "And whatever else may follow."

She fought the urge to down the whole glass. Her heart was pulsating so strongly that she was sure he could see it beneath her dress. With great restraint she took a small sip, swallowed and smiled, a breathless wave of heat consuming her.

As if sensing her discomfort, he redirected the conversation. "Mind if we just talk for a while?"

"N-no," she said. "That would be fine."

"Let me know when you want to start the fire—whenever you get hungry or feel a chill, okay?"

In her present state, she doubted either would happen tonight, but she nodded her head, anyway.

A family of velvet-antlered deer paused in front of the side window and Taylor and Josh watched them forage in silence. When they finally trailed off, Josh reclaimed Taylor's hand.

"I was wondering something," he said, easing gently into his subject. "This morning…before the plane arrived…you seemed troubled by something. Mind telling me what?"

She drank more wine and gathered her thoughts. Certainly she couldn't tell him about his father and her mother. Besides, what was there to tell? A fantasy does not an affair make. "I—I was thinking about Mom." She may have left out a few details, but this much was true.

"I thought that might be it." He squeezed her hand. "You must miss her terribly."

She set her goblet down next to his and gazed into his compassionate eyes. "Yes, I do. It's still hard to believe she's gone. Her birthday would have been next month, and yesterday I caught myself thinking about what to get her.''

Josh cupped Taylor's hand between both of his and she felt herself inching closer, staring at his lips, waiting for him to speak again, but wishing instead that his mouth was on hers.

''I do understand, you know.'' He glanced away for the first time and she let out a breath. ''I was a lot younger than you…about Billy's age…but I'll never forget the void I felt when my mother died.'' He fell silent for a moment, and she forgot about the kiss, sensing something revealing was about to be shared. ''Dad seemed in a world of his own, burying himself in work and the lecture circuit. He was rarely home. And when he was, it was only in body.''

Taylor could see the pain on Josh's face, as if it had happened only yesterday. Thank God she'd had longer with her mother. And had she been in Ann Arbor today, her father would be there, comforting her and sharing her grief. It didn't seem like Max not to have done the same. She couldn't help but wonder why he had handled things so poorly. But she wasn't about to speculate with Josh.

''It must have been pretty hard on you…being so young, I mean.''

He looked back at her and put on a brave front. ''Hannah was always there. She might sound gruff, but she gave us all plenty of hugs…as well as a few whoopin's whenever we needed them. But eventually it got to be too much for her…especially with Dad away so much. The hardest time was when we were all separated. For high school Ryder went to live with our aunt in Michigan…that's where he met Savannah, by the way. Shane was a senior and stayed here with our horse trainer, Buck, which is a story in itself that I'll save for another day. And I was shuffled off to Mom's parents in Denver.'' He shrugged, dismissing the added loneliness this must have caused them all. ''We got back together at the ranch a few years later. Except Ryder didn't stay long. Just the summer. When he left for college he never returned…not till a couple years ago.''

To look at the Malones now, she never would have guessed the problems they'd endured. Today they seemed like one big happy family.

"On that terrible day…it was Ryder who got home from school first." Josh swallowed hard. "He was the one who found her—"

Taylor held her breath, guessing what he was about to tell her.

"After she slit her wrists in the bathtub.''

Taylor didn't know what to say, so she said nothing, letting Josh take whatever time he needed. She struggled not to cry out loud. What worse betrayal than for an adored mother to abandon her young sons, especially the way she had? How sick she must have been.

And suddenly Josh's flitting from one woman to the next in college made perfect sense. How sad for them all, she thought, finally resting her head on the arm of Josh's chair and closing her eyes before he could see her tears.

Josh ran his hand over her hair for the longest time, saying nothing. The sun was low in the sky and the room had cooled significantly. She thought of starting the fire, but she didn't want to move. Something was happening in this quiet little space that only the two of them shared, an intimacy that she couldn't help but wonder if Josh had ever shared before; she knew she hadn't.

When he finally lifted her chin with his finger, she raised herself up on her knees, bringing her mouth inches from his. He met her the rest of the way, his kiss soft and light, first on her lips, then her cheek and neck.

Breathless, he stopped suddenly and pulled back, a look of sadness and longing sparring behind his eyes. "Maybe you'd better go.''

Confused, she sat back on her heels while he stared out at the dusky evening and didn't smile.

After an uncomfortable stretch of time, Taylor rubbed

her bare arms and stood. "Why do you want me to leave?" She tried to keep the tremor from her voice, but she was sure he heard it.

Finally he looked at her. "Let's just say I'm not very good at taking things slowly—"

She was about to take some of the responsibility when he added more.

"And I know you want more than I can give, Taylor."

She stared at his face to see if he was kidding. If he was, he hid it well. It was almost as though he was intentionally hurting her, driving her away.

As much as his words stung, she refused to let him see it. "Would you like me to start the fire before I leave?"

He shook his head and wheeled toward the bedroom without a backward glance. Taylor snatched her keys off the kitchen counter and left, not knowing what to think, too shaken to even try.

Josh heard the screen door bang shut and Taylor's car crunch over the gravel, and he wished he could call her back. He missed her already. Whatever had made him think he could take things slowly where Taylor was concerned? Now that he knew they could make love, he wanted her.

Tonight.

Badly.

He shook his head and muttered under his breath. "Stupid, stupid, stupid." One kiss and he wanted it all. And it wasn't simply physical; that was the problem. He cared too much for this woman.

And how selfish that was. He'd seen it coming and he'd done nothing to stop it. He'd seen the look in her eyes and knew she was beginning to care too much, too…in spite of his disabilities. He knew this wasn't his healthy ego talking, either. The evidence was in the generous and giving heart of Taylor that he had seen every time he'd looked deep into her eyes.

With both fists he pounded the sides of his legs and

growled in frustration. He couldn't saddle her with this. No matter how willing she might be to accept him as he was. She deserved more. Much more. And until he could give it to her, he had to bring a halt to feelings that were getting far too out of hand.

It had been nearly impossible to ask her to leave tonight. He doubted if he could ever muster the courage to do it again. So if he had to act like a jerk to keep from hurting her worse, so be it. He'd had plenty of practice at that.

Damn. Why wasn't the therapy working? He was told there was no permanent damage. If he were walking again, this night would have ended differently. He would be making love to Taylor this very moment...and assuring her she wasn't just another conquest. Already she meant more than any other woman he'd ever met. If only—

He beat his fist atop his right knee and his lower leg shot out, his foot falling off the footrest. He swore again, used both hands to reposition his leg and then stared out the window, for once not enjoying the view.

Hannah was dunking a tea bag into a china cup when Taylor dragged herself into the kitchen, feeling angry, confused, frustrated and, worst of all, thinking she'd made the grave mistake of falling for the wrong guy.

Hannah took one look at her and said, "That Joshua givin' you a hard time?" She moved the same tea bag to a second cup and poured steaming water from the kettle. "Come sit with me and have some tea. It's that herbal stuff Jenny made me switch to. No caffeine to keep ya tossin' and turnin' all night." She took both cups to the small table near the bay window and patted the seat next to her. Too tired to argue, Taylor dropped into the high-back chair and heaved a sigh.

"Talk to me, child. I'm a good listener." She let out a husky chortle. "And when yer all done, I love ta give advice."

Taylor couldn't help but smile. Maybe a good heart-to-heart might help. She couldn't feel much worse.

"Do ya like corn bread? Made some fresh this afternoon." Hannah didn't wait for an answer, but pushed herself out of the chair and ambled over to the cupboard. She came back with a plateful of cut squares and butter, depositing a plate and knife in front of each of them. She started spreading butter on hers and then waved her knife in Taylor's direction.

"Well? Ain't ya gonna eat some? Ya need more meat on them bones, child."

The bread did look good and her stomach was growling, so she did as she was told and wasn't sorry. "Umm. This is delicious. Haven't had corn bread since Mom—" she stopped chewing and sighed.

"Is that it, girl? Ya must miss yer mama somethin' awful." She reached over with her chubby, chafed hand and patted Taylor's arm.

Taylor took another sip of tea, thinking the question wasn't meant to be answered.

Hannah looked around as if to be certain they were alone, then she leaned forward and whispered. "Ya look jes like her, dear. Pretty as can be."

Stunned, Taylor set her teacup down and looked at Hannah.

"Maxwell showed me a picture of yer mama once. It was a newspaper clippin'...somethin' about the two gettin' some special award at your mama's hospital. They was real good friends back then, ya know. He always spoke real highly of her." Hannah picked up another piece of corn bread and averted her gaze.

Was Hannah trying to tell her something or was her overactive imagination at work again? Taylor took a bite of bread and watched the older woman out of the corner of her eye, hoping she would say more. But before she could, Jenny and Savannah strolled into the kitchen looking for something to eat. They spotted the corn bread, poured some tea and walked over to the table.

"We aren't interrupting anything, are we?" Jenny rubbed the small of her back, which only served to exaggerate the tight fit of her cotton top.

Taylor waved to the pair of empty seats. "No, no. Sit down. Please." Before you drop those babies where you stand, she thought. Taylor did a mental head shake, wondering how Jenny managed to walk with such a heavy load.

Jenny pulled out a chair and more or less slithered into it with a cat-that-ate-the-canary smile. "Out in the sun a lot today?" she asked, giving a sideways wink to Savannah.

"Now you two behave yerselves!" Hannah gave them a stern look and they both bit their top lips.

Taylor didn't consider herself dense, but she was definitely missing the joke. "Not really. Between the flight to Bozeman and two workouts, there wasn't time to spend outside."

Now the friends glanced at each other and burst into laughter.

Jenny gained control first. "Two workouts, huh?"

Taylor was becoming a little annoyed. "Yes. Two workouts."

"Then I guess that explains it."

Hannah reached across and slapped Jenny's hand as if she were a recalcitrant child, which only sent her into another round of giggles.

Savannah cleared her throat and looked somewhat contrite. "Sorry, Taylor. We're not really laughing at you. We've both been there...and believe me, we know it's not always funny."

"Excuse me, but what isn't always funny?"

Jenny ran her fingers across her cheek and down one side of her neck. "Whisker burns."

If Taylor's skin wasn't red before, it was now. She hadn't looked in the mirror since...since Josh had kissed her face and neck...with his coarse five-o'clock shadow. She was so caught up in things at the time, she hadn't even thought about it. Her fair skin irritated easily. She should have known.

Taylor picked up her tea, using the time to compose herself. As soon as she glanced up, Jenny stopped giggling and looked as though she might cry any second, a mood swing Taylor had seen at the hospital with more than one mama-to-be.

Jenny blinked hard before she spoke. "I'm sorry, sweetie. I must be getting pretty desperate for a laugh these days. I really didn't mean to embarrass you."

Taylor gave her a big smile, surprising them all. "If I can't take a little good-natured ribbing, I guess I'm living in the wrong house." She watched the tension evaporate around the table and knew she'd said the right thing. She leaned forward and placed both elbows on the table, feeling much better than when she'd arrived. "So tell me...what am I doing wrong? And how exactly did you manage to rope a couple of Malones?"

Hannah pushed out her chair. "Better cut some more bread and put another kettle on. Can see this ain't gonna be a quick one."

When the corn bread was gone, ice cream came next, and the women shared stories and laughed until exhaustion overtook them all. Hannah caved in first.

"I ain't no spring chicken, in case ya didn't notice." She tottered to her feet with difficulty. "I'm gonna hit the hay." She started for her room, then stopped to wag a finger at each of the three women. "Keep it down in here, now. These ol' bones need some sleep."

They said good-night, somewhat in unison, and then eyed each other before giving in to soft giggles once again.

"Now stop," Jenny said. "You're just going to force me to get up and go to the bathroom again."

Savannah cleared the table and came back. "I haven't had this much fun in ages." She rested a hand on Taylor's shoulder. "We might tease you, but we're so glad you care about Josh."

"Has it been that obvious?"

Savannah pointed to Taylor's neck. "Even before that."

Taylor chuckled and reflexively covered the chafed area with her hand. She didn't know how things would end up with Josh, but his sisters-in-law seemed pretty certain, which for now was enough to restore a little optimism.

Jenny propped an elbow on the table and said, "You know, we should probably be talking about the party since it's just around the corner." She rested her head in her palm, her eyelids starting to droop. "I've been cooking and freezing a few things, but I never heard a final count. Do we know yet?"

"Oh, that reminds me," Taylor said. "My dad and brother, Michael, will be flying in for a visit that weekend. Josh said to bring them."

"Super!" Savannah said. "Can't wait to meet them." She squinted her eyes and started counting on her fingers. "That should make about forty or so. Nice-size group."

"Speaking of flying," Jenny said, circling her free hand over her bulging middle, "how did Josh do today?"

"Like he never missed a beat. The hand controls worked like a charm."

"Whew! That's a relief." Jenny pushed both palms down on the table and hauled herself out of the chair. "I don't want an instant replay of Savannah's delivery, that's for sure. Give me a hospital and drugs and I'll be a happy camper."

Taylor gazed at Savannah, who was smiling up at Jenny. "You mean you didn't have either?" Taylor asked, thinking she must have misunderstood.

Jenny chuckled and waddled toward the hallway. "That's a story for another night." She stopped suddenly and frowned. "Maybe I should ask Grandma to come stay here just in case."

"Is this one of your clairvoyant things or simple para-noia?" Savannah asked.

"I don't know…just know I'd feel better if Grandma was close by."

"There's always Max in a pinch," Savannah offered.

Jenny wrinkled her nose. "Your father-in-law delivering your baby? Not my first choice. Think I'll talk to Grandma at the party." She started back down the hall. "See you guys in the morning."

Taylor stood and pushed in her chair, eyeing Savannah with new admiration. "You had little Chris here? At the ranch?"

She nodded and looked proud. "Without Max or Ryder or drugs."

"No! Really?"

"Yep. The guys were in Bozeman at a banquet and I was a month early. Jenny read instructions from one of Max's books and her grandmother delivered."

"But her grandmother is a nurse or something, right?"

Savannah laughed as she stood. "Or something. She's a very wise old Crow Indian, that's who she is." She hiked up her eyebrows. "Oh! and she and Buck will be at Josh's party, too, so you can meet them."

"Buck? You mean the one who used to be the horse trainer?"

"Yep. He married Jenny's grandmother, Mary Howls at the Moon." Savannah put an arm around Taylor's shoulder. "I forgot…you *have* missed a lot." She gave Taylor a hug. "Let's do this again. We'll tell you all about them then."

Taylor hugged her back, feeling as though she were already part of the family. If only things were as easy with Josh. "I had a good time tonight," she said.

"Me, too, sweetie." Savannah turned to go, then paused. "Good luck with Josh tomorrow. Oh, and I'm so glad we'll get to meet your family at the party. Night."

Taylor said good-night and climbed the stairs to her room.

I'm so glad we'll get to meet your family at the party.
Why did the idea still bother her? Nothing had really happened between Mom and Max. And both Dad and Max were mature men.

Then what could possibly go wrong at the party?

Twelve

There was very little eye contact as they struggled through the morning workout. If Taylor was looking at his face, Josh didn't notice.

He was tired and hot and totally frustrated. In more ways than one. It was impossible to be just friends with this woman. And his useless legs made anything more out of the question. Whatever made him think he could work so closely with her and not lose his mind?

This was ridiculous, he told himself. What difference did one stupid session make? None of it was doing any good, anyway. With his arms quivering on the bars, he lowered himself to the mat and, breathing heavily, stretched out on his back.

"Forget it. I'm whipped," he said, staring at the ceiling.

Taylor paced the length of the mat, her own breathing growing louder. He knew she was priming herself for battle, but he didn't care. He'd fooled himself long enough.

He wasn't going to walk again. No matter how hard he tried.

Taylor stopped alongside him and balled her fists at her waist. "Fine. Lie there and rot. See if I care."

He glanced at her, but didn't move. "Oh, you care. That tough act doesn't fool me."

She started pacing again. "Is that right?"

"You care too much, that's your problem."

She stopped and glowered down at him. "Did anyone ever tell you you're an arrogant son of a bitch?"

He curled his lip and chuckled. "Oh, yeah. Many times. You just noticing?"

"Errr!" She strode to the kitchen and he heard the water running in the sink, then a glass slammed down on the counter.

He blew out a few calming breaths and locked his hands behind his head. When she returned he said, "You know…your frustration has less to do with my legs than your own lust."

She stepped closer to his head, her chest rising and falling rapidly, looking as though she would like to slap him if he were at her level, or maybe kick him where it hurt. But what good would that do? He wouldn't feel it.

She spun around and he knew she was about to walk out the door. And in that instant he hated her for her ability to do so. She walked alongside him and had nearly cleared the mat when his right foot reached out and tripped her, sending her sprawling on all fours with a loud thud.

Josh rose on his elbows and felt the panic in his chest when she didn't move. "Taylor? Talk to me. I'm so sorry. I didn't mean to—"

She sat up quickly and stared openmouthed at his foot. "You tripped me?"

"I'm so sorry. I—" The realization of what had happened struck him like an electrical charge. "How did I do that?"

She was still staring at his foot. "Try it again."

He did, but nothing happened. She removed his shoe and sock and tossed them aside.

"Wiggle your toes."

Josh closed his eyes and concentrated with all his might. *Please, God, let this be the moment.*

He kept praying and focusing on his right foot until suddenly he cried out, "Ouch!" He looked down and saw Taylor grinning from ear to ear. "What was that?" he asked.

"I just pinched your big toe. You had it coming." She starting massaging his foot, and the touch of her warm hands on his skin almost brought him to tears. He could feel it. He could actually feel it. He wiggled his toes again and watched what seemed like a miracle. Just when he'd given up....

He started to laugh, and then so did Taylor. She set his foot down on the mat and moved closer, her laughter fading as she met his steady gaze. Without another word, she wrapped her arms around his neck and rocked him from side to side.

Josh closed his eyes and thanked God—for this miracle and for bringing Taylor into his life. He held her tight and rocked with her, thinking life was good, that he'd never felt happier than at this moment.

But then her mouth met his and his happiness soared to a new dimension. She stopped and pulled back, looking suddenly wary.

"Are you going to ask me to leave again?"

He shook his head slowly, seeing the uncertainty in her eyes. "I—I wasn't sure this would happen.... I wanted more for you, Taylor." He watched a sheen settle over her eyes.

"And now?"

He looked at his toes and back to her. "I'm going to walk, aren't I?"

She smiled and tried to sound tough. "If I have anything

to do with it.'' She inched closer, her gaze on his mouth. ''About this taking things slowly—''

He indulged one husky laugh, that seemed to start from his glorious toes and push past the lump in his throat. Then he pulled her to him and took her lips greedily and she met each thrust of his tongue. He tore at her clothes as savagely as she did his, each article thrown frantically aside. He still couldn't feel when her hands trailed below his waist, but he had no doubt what she would find this time. Excitement didn't begin to describe what he was feeling when her tongue licked his earlobes and then quickly found its way back to his mouth.

Josh gripped her face in both his hands and held her away from him, trying with his eyes to tell her how much he cared. He scrutinized every line and curve of her mouth, her eyes, her cheeks, her lips. She was beautiful. Inside and out. What had he ever done to deserve this perfect creature? He opened his mouth to speak, but words could not do justice to what he felt.

Tears trickled down her flushed cheeks and he wiped them away with the pads of his thumbs, knowing they were from joy and hopefully something greater. But he wasn't ready to ask how deep her feelings ran, to risk hearing anything short of the answer he wanted. So he pulled her back to him, and this time their kiss was slow and gentle. Hunger and greed were replaced with giving, each aiming to please the other, to find that special, intimate spot never pleasured before.

She slid her knees down to the mat on either side of his hips and locked her arms next to his chest, brushing her inner thighs along the length of him, her eyes rolling back as a moan escaped from deep in her throat.

He raised his head and watched as she positioned herself over him and took him inside her. He marveled at how much pleasure he derived from something he couldn't yet feel. Though he knew that sometime soon he would, and he imagined the moment in his mind, keeping himself erect for as long as she wanted him.

And oh, how she wanted him.

The passion and pleasure on her face burned her cheeks with such an intensity that, with great difficulty, he sat up and touched her face with one hand and held her tight around the waist with the other. Her full, firm breasts pressed against him and he groaned into her ear. "Taylor, my sweet, beautiful Taylor."

She helped him onto his back again and then slid her hands beneath his bottom and raised him to her, grinding her hips harder and faster, her breathing hot and loud in his ear. Their tongues imitated the rhythm of her movements, and soon she was shuddering against his chest, his hands gliding up and down her slick back, spreading the intimacy of their kiss.

Her breathing slowed and she raised herself up on one elbow, gazed into his eyes and then kissed him gently.

He reached up and kissed her nose, then collapsed to the mat with a happy chuckle. "So much for taking it slow, huh?"

Taylor smiled down at him and eyed him longingly.

He reached up and tucked strands of wavy blond hair behind her ears, then brushed her cheek with the back of his hand, trying to convey words he wasn't ready to say. More had to happen before he could tell her his true feelings. A toe wiggle was a long way from walking. And that had to come first. Soon, he hoped. Very soon.

"Are we expecting anyone?" She asked, out of the blue. He frowned, not understanding the question. "Should we hurry up and get dressed or can we lie around naked for a while?"

Josh let out a hearty laugh, the biggest he could remember in ages. "If you're so worried, you could always shut and lock the doors and come back."

He didn't have to ask twice. With less inhibition than he would have guessed, she made her way from the front of the house to the side door and back as he cupped his hands behind his head and enjoyed the scenery. She set the small oscillating fan from the kitchen on the floor near the mat, plugged it in and then lay down on the mat beside him.

"Ahhh," she said, resting her head in the crook of his arm. "Don't know why I didn't think of this earlier."

He laughed and tugged her closer to him. "Fan or no fan, it still would have been hot in here, my love."

She lifted her head and stared at him a moment, then smiled and snuggled down next to him.

Two days later, Taylor made the trek to Bozeman. After meeting with her stand-in and a few patients, she stopped by the apartment for mail and phone messages. She was eager to return to the farm and Josh. His progress had been remarkable, and the bond that had begun to be forged between them was doubly exciting.

She stuffed a couple of bills in her purse and noticed the steady red light on the answering machine. Good. No calls. If she hurried, she could be back for a short session with Josh before dinner.

She stared at the phone one last time and then raced to it. Maybe Dad or Michael were home for lunch and she could catch them. Dad answered on the third ring.

"Taylor! I'm so glad you called. I was going to call you tonight and give you our arrival time."

"Just a sec. Let me find a pencil." She wrote the time and did a quick calculation. If the flight wasn't late, they could drop luggage off here, then get to the farm before the party started. She wanted the men to have a little time getting to know each other before the crowd arrived.

"Sorry we could only get seats on the Fourth. Everything else was booked."

"No problem, Dad. I'll be there."

"Just ten more days. Can't wait to see you, sweetheart."

"Me, neither, Dad."

She hung up, having decided before not to make a big

deal of the party. She would tell them on the way home from the airport.

She locked up the apartment and ran down the stairs and to her car. On the long drive back she thought about the best way to handle things once they arrived. She would tell them she was taking them to a big ranch and farm that had livestock and horses. That would get Michael excited. Then she would add that the party was that night...and there would be fireworks, too.

She nodded her head, thinking it was a good plan. Both her dad and Michael were spontaneous-type people who liked surprises. She would assure them that they would have plenty of alone time later.

But maybe she wouldn't mention that the party was at the Malones until they were on the way to Joeville. If she was driving, she wouldn't be able to see her father's reaction. Maybe it was selfish, but she didn't want to know if he'd ever surmised her mom's crush on Max. Besides, there would be such a crowd at the farm that, except for quick introductions, her dad wouldn't have to talk with Max the rest of the night.

Yes, she told herself. Everything would work out fine. Surely Josh and Dad and Michael would hit it off.

The rest would take care of itself.

Just about every Malone vehicle was in Josh's driveway when Taylor arrived late that afternoon. Panic overtook her and she ran from her car not bothering to shut the door. Did he fall? What had happened?

She pushed through the door and raced to the parlor where the family stood in a circle around Josh. Her tennis shoes squeaked to a halt on the hardwood floor and she exhaled a loud breath.

Josh smiled over the heads of Jenny and Savannah. "Glad you could make the party. Check this out." With a struggle he moved his right leg a small step forward, his arms still doing most of the work on the bars. The family hooted and clapped and encouraged him on. He paused a moment for a deep breath, then took another small step with his left leg.

Taylor watched from behind the family, her heart so full she thought it would burst. More than anything, she wanted to run to Josh and throw her arms around him. But this moment wasn't about her...or even them. It was Josh's moment in the spotlight and he deserved it. It had been a long, hard struggle—and it wasn't over yet—but she had little doubt he would make it to the end now.

A moment of insecurity caught her breath and she stood rooted in place. In school she'd been taught to watch for patients becoming too attached to their caregivers, misinterpreting feelings of gratitude for more. She'd even seen evidence of this at the hospital from time to time. Now she couldn't help but wonder: had Josh been drawn to her mainly because she was a therapist who was helping him get back on his feet? When the job was done, would she be gone from here and soon forgotten?

And beyond all that, was the Joshua Malone, who had confided in her about the horror and pain surrounding his mother's suicide, ready for a real commitment?

Josh looked back at her and beamed, and she pushed such morbid thoughts from her head. Only time would answer such questions. Besides, this was a day for celebration.

Taylor blew him a kiss when she thought no one was looking, but Ryder let out a wolf whistle.

"Hot damn," he said, grinning at Taylor. "Looks like lots of good things have been happening around here lately." He winked at Josh. "Congratulations, little bro."

Josh didn't acknowledge his brother, but continued eyeing Taylor, which caused every head to turn in her direction. Embarrassed, she placed both hands in front of her face, but couldn't resist a small chuckle from behind her limited cover. She braved a peek between her fingers in time to catch Hannah and Max exchanging a sly look, acting as if they had orchestrated this whole affair.

Finally she dropped her hands and gave up, crossing to her favorite patient, who was waiting for a hug. She gave it to him, along with a peck on the cheek, and ignored the playful rowdiness around them. They all seemed so sure she was part of Josh's future. She closed her eyes and hugged him again and prayed that they were right.

Workouts were grueling and recovery slower than he'd hoped, but Josh could see light at the end of the tunnel. Yet he sensed a certain reserve from Taylor ever since a week ago when he took those first steps. She'd told him that he had to save his energy for therapy, that it was best that other activities be put on hold a little longer. Even though they didn't make love again, they didn't argue, either. If she wanted him to work longer on a particular day, he worked longer. If she suggested he try a new procedure, he did as he was told. It was almost as though they were strictly therapist and patient, except he knew there was more between them, just waiting to be explored.

Maybe she knew him well enough by now to know that he had to be whole before their relationship could move forward. Whatever her reason, it motivated him to try harder. He ate up her words of encouragement like a starving man and drank in her sweet smiles and tender touches, never getting his fill.

Taylor had to feel the same as he did, Josh decided. He could wait. It wouldn't be long now.

Saturday was the big party, only three days off, and Taylor left early to help Jenny and Savannah with last minute arrangements. Josh drank iced tea at the kitchen table and thought about his own private plans for that night. During all the hours of therapy, when he and Taylor didn't speak of personal things, Josh's mind as well as his body was busy.

There was no doubt that Taylor was the woman for him. He'd probably known it since day one, only now he didn't resist the idea. He finished off his tea and waited for Hank to help him with his nightly routine. All he had to do was get onto crutches by the night of the Fourth to convince himself he wasn't rushing things. If he could manage that, he would proceed with the rest of his plan. He would need a little help, but he knew someone in the family would jump at the chance.

He smiled and watched a strong wind whip the tops of the trees, feeling a storm in the air. He closed his eyes and pictured himself with Taylor walking in the rain, hand in hand, and he sighed.

Maybe during the fireworks with the light sparkling on her beautiful face. Yes. He liked that idea.

Saturday would be the perfect night. Even her dad and brother would be there; everyone who mattered to both of them would be present.

He massaged both of his legs with his hands, grateful that he could now feel the results. "Come on, legs. Just a little more by Saturday," he whispered. "I know you can do it."

Thirteen

It didn't happen Thursday, but on Friday afternoon, with Taylor on one side and Max on the other, Josh took his first tentative steps on crutches. Like an oasis, the wheelchair seemed miles away, when in fact it was ten feet straight ahead.

Josh's breathing was labored and his arms felt as though they were about to buckle under the strain, but inch by inch he made his way closer, beads of sweat dripping down his temples, back and chest. Once there, he began the tedious process of turning, which took almost as long as the journey from the bars. Finally he dropped with a whoosh into the wheelchair. He puffed out his cheeks a few times and sucked in air before raising his gaze to the pair of beaming faces in front of him.

Tears trickled down Taylor's rosy cheeks and his father's eyes brimmed with moisture. Josh could feel their jubilation, though it couldn't come close to his own. He smiled at them both and savored the moment. There was something delicious about the secret he harbored from both of them. Though they would know soon enough.

He had met his first goal with the crutches. If he worked fast, there was still time to meet the next.

The phone rang and Josh reached out for Taylor's hand. "Mind taking that for me in the kitchen? If it's urgent, bring the portable back, okay?" She darted off and Josh motioned his father closer.

"Dad...there's something I need you to help me with...but you can't tell Taylor."

Max hunkered down beside the chair and Josh spelled out the details quickly. Max told him Hannah could help and he agreed to talk to her.

Then Taylor stepped back into the parlor and Josh changed the subject.

"Yep. Hank was able to fix the faulty unit with parts from the one in the fire. What a gem that guy is. And he never complains helping me shower or all the other junk jobs I throw his way. As soon as I can swing it, I told him he was due for a raise." Taylor took his hand and squeezed it before sitting on the floor beside him. "Was that call for me?" he asked.

"No. Actually it was for me...my brother. He's so excited." She laughed, looking every bit as enthused. "He wanted to tell me their flight number was changed. He doesn't realize there are only two gates and I couldn't miss them if I tried."

"Will they make it in time for the party?" Josh asked.

"I sure hope so...if their plane's on time. They're bringing carry-ons only, so that will speed things up. It would be nice if you had a little time to visit with them before everyone else got here."

He peered down at her, barely able to contain his own excitement. If only she knew what he had in store for her. "Even if they're late, I'll make time. I can't wait to meet them." She stroked his arm and gazed up at him in a way that made him feel ten feet tall.

Max moved toward the window, distracting Josh from his dream and bringing him back to the real world. Something seemed wrong. His father's back was to them and his head was bent pensively. Only minutes ago he was ecstatic. Now he looked as though he had the weight of the world on his shoulders.

Josh glanced down at Taylor, who was resting her head on his arm and enjoying one of their few reprieves. He stroked her hair and wondered what was going on in his father's head. Yet he knew better than to ask, especially with anyone else around.

His father was a very private and sometimes secretive person. Josh made a mental note to ask what was wrong the next time they were alone.

Maybe on Sunday.

After the party.

While she waited for the plane to land, Taylor wondered if her burgeoning feelings for Josh were transparent, if her father would see the change in her and know the excitement and tenderness she felt in her heart. She tried to remember exactly when she stopped fighting the truth. But before she could pinpoint the moment, she spotted the plane taxiing to the gate, and suddenly she felt like a little girl at Christmas. For years she had waited for this day—to show her father and Michael her beloved Montana. Now they would realize why she and her mother had loved this place so very much. And before long they would come to know the man who had stolen her heart.

Michael was first through the gate, his smile almost as wide as the arms that spread out to greet her. He rocked her from side to side and they both laughed from the pure joy of being together. Her father looked on from behind, and Taylor pulled him into their embrace, kissing his cheek and holding him tight. She thought he looked thinner, but then he smiled, and she knew the next few days would be ones that they would never forget.

"How was your flight?" she asked, stepping back from the pair, holding their hands.

Michael acted the part of a seasoned traveler, which she thought was amusing, but she listened to him prattle on about every little detail as they walked down the stairs and out to her car.

When he finally took a breath, Taylor said, "My apartment isn't far. We'll be there in a few minutes." She was glad she had to keep her eyes on the highway now that it was time to tell them the rest. "Did you get any sleep on the plane?"

Michael laughed. "Dad snored most of the way. I poked him when I saw the mountains, and he opened one eye for a few seconds." Taylor glanced at the rearview mirror, and her father was nodding and smiling. Michael continued. "I didn't sleep a wink, but I'm not at all tired. Why? Got something in mind for today?"

"Well, yes. If Dad's up to it."

Her father leaned forward and folded his arms against the top of the seat back. "We haven't got long, so better get started."

She sighed a breath of relief. The first hurdle had been crossed. "There's a party tonight—lots of good food, fireworks, horses—"

Michael interrupted on cue. "Horses? That we can ride?"

"I'm sure that could be arranged."

"Cool. So when do we leave?"

"I thought we'd stop by my apartment first. You can freshen up and change if you want, then we can go...if it's okay with Dad."

"Whatever you want, sweetheart. I'm just happy we're together."

"Me, too, Dad." She turned into her parking lot thinking, So far, so good.

The men carried their bags up, complimented her sparse digs and then took turns in the shower. Dad went first and

Michael followed. From behind the bathroom door, Michael shouted out, "Any unattached females going to be there?"

Taylor rolled her eyes. "Maybe. I'm not sure." She thought of joking about the ladies from the Purple Palace whom Billy had invited, but she bit her tongue. Even though she didn't approve of their profession, Billy loved the motley group who had helped his mother, Maddy, raise him. Besides, they were probably all too old for Michael's liking, anyway.

She checked the clock over the stove. "What's taking you so long?"

"Decided to shave again. Be out in a sec."

Her father sat patiently at the kitchen table, looking out the window, not saying a word in typical dad-fashion.

She walked over to him. "Want some instant iced tea? Afraid that's all I've got to offer."

He glanced at her and smiled. "Water would be fine."

"Coming right up." She was emptying an ice tray when Michael started swearing from the bathroom. The door opened and he walked out with a bloody towel pressed to his neck.

"Michael!" She set the tray down and rushed to him, lifting the towel away from his neck and inspecting the damage.

"It's okay, sis. It was a new blade. Cut myself shaving. It's the towel I'm worried about. Look." He held it out for her to see. What was once clean and creamy colored, was now blotched with big dark stains.

"Don't be silly. It's just a towel." She wet a section of paper toweling and pressed it to his cut. "Here, use this." Then she snatched the soiled towel and tossed it into the sink. "I'll take care of it later. Now, let's get going, okay?"

"Should I wear a T-shirt or a button-down?" he asked, walking back to the mirror and checking for fresh blood.

Grrr. "A T-shirt with nothing weird on it." He was combing his hair again. What could she do to hurry him up? "It takes about two hours to get there, you know. Hope we're not too late for the horses."

Two minutes later the men crawled back into the car and Taylor sped off. They headed west on Interstate 90 and Michael kept up a steady stream of questions about each site they caught a glimpse of—the Absaroka Mountain Range, the Yellowstone River, Prairie Dog Town. They were more than halfway there and Taylor still hadn't worked up the courage to mention the name of the family hosting the party. Then Michael made her job easier.

"Is this a dude ranch we're going to?"

She laughed and expelled a long breath before explaining. "Well, it's not really a ranch where we're going. It's an old farmhouse on hundreds of acres of gorgeous land." She glanced over and was relieved that he didn't seem disappointed.

"What's the difference?"

Her father answered from the back seat. "Ranchers raise cattle. Farmers raise crops." He sounded proud to know. "Your mama told me that years ago."

Michael eyed her suspiciously. "But they do have horses, right?"

"Yes, Michael. They do have horses." At twenty, he was only five years her junior, yet at times like this she appreciated the difference. She smiled and caught a similar look on her father's face in the rearview mirror.

It was now or never, she thought. "If time allows, maybe you could ride a horse over to the ranch and look at the cattle. This is a large compound we're going to...fourth-generation land that runs for miles...lots of outbuildings, wildlife, wilderness."

"Cool."

Michael was satisfied, but she wasn't done with the job yet. With her eyes on the highway ahead, she struggled to keep her tone as casual as before. "Actually, the land belongs to the family I work for. Remember the plane crash I told you about?"

"Uh-huh."

"Well, the patient who got injured in it is a friend of mine." And, oh, so much more. "He's the son of the doctor whose clinic I work in part-time."

"Oh, yeah," he said. "Mom's old friend from U of M Hospital, right? What was his name?"

"Malone." She wanted to glance in the mirror, again, but she didn't dare. "Josh Malone is the one in therapy...he owns the farm. The party is sort of a housewarming." Why was this making her so tense? Her mouth felt like a desert, and she couldn't swallow. "I thought you and Dad would enjoy the property and especially the house. It's over a hundred years old, and Josh did most of the restoring himself. Finished it shortly before the accident. When I told him you were both carpenters, he couldn't wait for you to come."

She was rambling and she knew it, but at last the words that she had dreaded ever since she'd learned they were coming were finally out. Now she did a mental head shake and wondered why she'd put herself through all this unnecessary angst. After all, it was important that her family meet Josh...the man who might some day be...

She smiled and relaxed behind the wheel, leaving the thought dangling, not wanting to jinx her secret dream. When she finally checked the rearview mirror, her father was watching a pair of pronghorn antelope on the ridge straight ahead, apparently indifferent to the conversation up front.

She'd been silly to worry.

They were the first to arrive as Taylor had planned. And just as she'd hoped, the three men hit it off right from the start. She found it next to impossible to keep her eyes off Josh's smiling face while the men talked easily about the farm and its history. She wondered if her father noticed how much Josh obviously meant to her. If he did, he didn't let on. He seemed in a fairly good mood and even let Michael have a beer when Josh offered. She knew it wasn't her brother's first, but it probably was in front of his dad.

Josh showed off the lower level, not seeming at all self-conscious of the wheelchair. Taylor volunteered to give the tour of the second floor, which her father and Michael inspected more carefully out of Josh's sight.

"He really did a great job," Michael whispered, sounding surprised. "I thought you said he was a farmer."

She laughed and felt proud as she led them back downstairs, where Hannah, Jenny and Savannah had arrived and were setting out appetizers around the house.

After introductions the women returned to their tasks and Taylor joined them, watching from afar when her father walked over to Josh. He patted Josh's shoulder and she heard him say, "Fine job, Josh. Fine job."

"Coming from a professional, Mr. Phillips, that's a real compliment. Thanks."

"John…call me John."

A sheen settled over Taylor's eyes and she blinked hard. She had worried needlessly. This was working out far better than she had ever hoped.

Hannah bustled into the room and held out a tray to the two men. "Mind if I call ya John, too? My name's Hannah. Do the housekeepin' back at the ranch." She nodded with the top of her head in the general direction.

"Please do," John said, and took a cheese puff off the tray.

"Lots more where this came from. We got us a real good cook." She glanced at the doorway as Jenny waddled through. "This is her now…Jenny. She's married to that big galoot behind her, Shane."

Taylor hung back as everything unfolded in front of her, keeping an eye on her father, seeing nothing amiss and enjoying the glow on Josh's face. She heard Shane say Max had an emergency at the clinic and would be along later, and Taylor sighed with relief. The idea of a crowded room sounded easier when the time actually came for Dad and

Max to meet, though now she was beginning to believe it wouldn't be a problem, anyway.

Hank came in and was quick to volunteer a horse and company for Michael and the pair disappeared. Ryder, Savannah, Billy and baby Chris joined the cluster soon after, and before long friends and family filled every nook and cranny, some spilling over onto the porch out front or the yard, where coals were being piled high in grills.

While many of the men offered up their prized secrets for barbecuing, the women fussed over every imaginable dish. Taylor couldn't remember seeing so much food in one place at one time. Platters of steaks passed in front of her on their way to and from the grills, eventually finding a place on the massive table in the dining room as everyone queued up for the feast.

Still more people streamed in and Josh greeted each guest with more warmth and enthusiasm than Taylor ever recalled seeing. Before the accident, he'd always been a happy-go-lucky sort, but she thought there was much more to this man now. More depth and maturity. Or had she finally opened her eyes to what was there all along?

Occasionally she and Josh would make eye contact and his smile would broaden. A private look would pass between them and then it was gone as another guest would block their view. More than once she toyed with the idea of offering her dad and Michael use of her car so she could spend the night with Josh, but each time she dismissed it, feeling selfish. Her family was here for such a short visit. She and Josh had all the time in the world. Yet for some reason, tonight seemed so right to tell him how she felt. If ever they could find a moment alone.

Michael returned from his ride, breathless and flushed with excitement, and Taylor decided once and for all that her personal plans with Josh must wait.

She looked around for her father and saw him sitting with Billy on the front steps. Three women of various shapes and ages were shaking Dad's hand, while he did his best not to appear stunned. Taylor watched at the screen door and Michael joined her.

"Whoa!" he said, at seeing the garish trio. "Is that how they dress around here?"

Taylor chuckled softly, not wanting to draw attention. "That's how they dress at the Purple Palace."

Michael swallowed his potato salad and nearly dropped his plate. "No sh—" He closed his mouth and openly stared. "You mean they live at one of those places where...you know." Taylor nodded and Michael looked again. "I kind of like the youngest one in the short black leather skirt. Think I should go introduce myself?"

Taylor slanted him a grin. "*Introduce* would be nice."

"Isn't Billy a little young for friends like these?"

Taylor's grin disappeared. "He lived with these women...until his mother died. She ran the place."

"Gee. Poor kid."

Taylor hooked her arm behind her brother's elbow. "Ryder and Savannah adopted him. Josh told me the little guy still misses his home and the girls...and his mom, of course. But he seems to have adjusted fairly well."

Michael was silent a moment. "Have you?"

She knew he was referring to their own mother, and out of the blue the journals popped into her head. She wondered if she would ever tell him they existed. Maybe someday. When more time had passed. It had been hard enough on her, reading them; she didn't want to—

"Sis?" He slipped an arm around her shoulder and she remembered his question.

"I miss her. A lot. Time is helping, though. And you?"

He squeezed her tight. "Same here."

Billy tugged at one of the women's hands and all three marched through the front door, bracelets jangling, false eyelashes batting, and Michael followed them to the food area without as much as a "see you later." Taylor laughed and turned just as Jenny made her way over, an elderly pair close behind. Members of the Crow tribe, Taylor guessed, having met several at the hospital.

Jenny caught her breath, her huge middle looking as though she'd swallowed whole one of the watermelons Taylor had seen in the kitchen. Jenny hooked arms with the old woman and the man came alongside.

"Taylor Phillips, this is my grandmother, Mary Howls at the Moon, and her husband, Bucking Horse. Buck used to train the horses at the ranch for years." She winked sideways at her grandmother. "Until this sexy lady stole him away from us. Now they live at Crow Agency."

Mary elbowed her granddaughter, then said, "Nice to meet you, Taylor Phillips. My Jenny say you give good medicine to Joshua."

Jenny threw an arm around Mary's small shoulders and beamed. "This is the other great medicine woman around here...the one I told you about."

Finally it dawned on Taylor who she was talking with. "Oh, yes. The one who delivered Savannah's baby! It's great to meet you...both of you."

"Speaking of which," Jenny said. "Any chance you two could stay with us until these babies are born?" She rubbed her belly and winced. "Just in case things happen too fast or Josh isn't here to fly us to the hospital."

Taylor watched the old couple share a private glance, then Buck smiled and answered Jenny's question. "Éeh. We thought you never ask."

"Oh, thank you." She gave them each a peck on the cheek. "What a load off my mind. I'll be right back. I want to find Shane and tell him."

Taylor was eager to learn about the emergency delivery as well as life on the reservation and was happy to be left alone with the interesting pair. She stepped closer and then froze.

Max's familiar voice came from the front porch. She turned and looked.

Her father was still sitting on the top step.

Alone.

Fourteen

Taylor watched as Max extended a hand to her father. She started toward them, but suddenly Buck clasped both his callused hands over hers and held her tight. She tried to listen to what Buck was saying—something about horses and other trivial matters—but her concentration was on the pair shaking hands on the porch. She could vaguely hear Max expressing his condolences and she noticed that her dad looked away. In itself it meant nothing since she'd seen him do this before whenever her mother's passing flowed into the conversation. If only she could see his face. But Buck seemed intent on holding fast to her hand, and now Mary was talking to her, too.

The moment on the porch passed and her father came inside, his face appearing more fatigued. It had been a long day for him, she told herself. He spotted her and she waved him over. As she slid an arm around his back, Buck introduced himself and Mary. Soon Ryder wheeled Josh over and they joined in the conversation—a little about the house, a lot about all the great food. Small talk. Nice and safe. And once again Taylor began to relax. Max and Dad had met—whether for the first time or not, she may never know—but at least from what she could tell it had gone okay.

Josh looked across the circle at her and held her gaze, ignoring everyone else around them. Not too long ago she may have thought that taking her to bed was the only thing on his mind. Now his eyes said something else, something far more personal, meaningful.

Ryder penetrated her fog when he asked, "Taylor, I don't think anyone told me how you ended up in Montana."

She forced her gaze away from Josh and looked at Ryder, her inner smile most likely showing. "My mom was raised out here…went to Montana State for her nursing degree."

"A nurse? Not a physical therapist like you?"

"I started with nursing, too. Then I saw some of the great things your dad was doing and I went in another direction. There seemed a great need for aftercare and—" she shrugged "—well, here I am."

Josh nudged his brother. "I thought I told you. Dad and Taylor's mom worked together in Ann Arbor. They were good friends when Dad was there."

Taylor watched the color drain from Ryder's face and an alarm sounded in her head. Suddenly he didn't know where to look. He twisted the beer bottle in his hand, glanced at Buck briefly and then said, "Excuse me. Think I'll see if Savannah needs a break from the baby."

Taylor looked from Mary to Buck, who were both staring at their feet, then to Josh, who seemed oblivious to anything or anyone but her. Had she imagined it? Or had something significant just transpired?

Buck took Mary's hand and soon they were lost in the crowd, leaving Taylor alone with Josh. She was debating whether to ask him what he thought that was all about when Billy rushed up.

"Uncle Josh…when do the fireworks start?"

Josh pulled the boy to him and chuckled. "I can't wait, either, Billy. Soon as it's dark. Won't be long now. Why don't you go help Hank set things up?"

Billy darted from the room and again they were alone. The way Josh was looking up at her stole her breath away, making her forget earlier worries. What could be wrong when things were so right between her and this special man? She stepped closer to him. "Josh…I—"

He held an index finger to his lips and said softly, "Let's wait for the fireworks, okay?"

She nodded silently as Savannah and Hannah entered the room with large trays of assorted beverages and wound their way through the crowd. When all had a glass, Max clanked a spoon to his and asked for everyone's attention. Taylor pulled a chair alongside Josh, and he held her hand, his gaze saying more than she'd ever seen before. If she had any doubts how she felt about this man, looks like this were quickly dispelling them. She thought she could drown in the love and admiration she saw there. And suddenly she wished she hadn't agreed to wait to tell him she felt the same way.

Max spoke loudly over the din of glasses and utensils. "I'd like to thank everyone for coming today and the ladies for all the terrific food." There was a thunderous round of applause and words of praise, but still Taylor held Joshua's gaze. "And to my son, Joshua…for the outstanding work he did on this old place—" more applause and cheers "—and his bravery throughout his ordeal. He probably hasn't been boasting, so I will. Yesterday Josh started walking on crutches." Excited conversations danced around the house and Taylor kissed the back of Josh's hand adoringly, no longer concerned about rumors or what others thought. He mouthed the words "thank you" before everyone crushed closer. Taylor squeezed his hand, then let go and stood, giving Josh center stage.

And in that instant she saw her father. Sitting on the far

side of the room. Elbows on knees, his face white and sullen, making him look deathly ill. She nudged her way to him and knelt at his feet. He didn't meet her gaze.

"Dad! What's wrong?"

Still staring at the space between his knees, he said. "It's been a long day. I—I'm exhausted."

"I should take you back to the apartment."

He looked up, his eyes as sad as the day of her mother's death. "I don't want to ruin your fun."

"Nonsense. Let me find Michael. You stay put." She patted his knee, wondering if she should take him to the hospital instead. He seemed more than exhausted; he seemed physically ill.

She spotted Michael on the far side of the crowd and was making her way to him when she heard the breaking of plates and a sudden frenzy coming from the kitchen.

Shane shouted, "Dad! The kitchen."

Max was just ahead of her and Taylor followed him, hoping it was nothing serious, thinking she might be able to help. She stopped in the doorway when she saw the problem. Max knelt on the floor beside Jenny and was talking soothingly into her ear. Jenny said something Taylor couldn't quite hear, but it didn't take a rocket scientist to figure out what was happening.

Max stood and spotted Taylor. "Tell Josh to get himself ready to fly to Bozeman. We may not have a lot of time."

The normally calm Shane looked worse than Jenny. "Someone find Mary. Jenny wants her grandmother with her."

Ryder helped Josh down the ramp and into the nearest car while Taylor escorted a nervous Mary to the back seat where Max and Jenny were waiting. Shane was behind the wheel looking ready to shout if another thirty seconds were wasted before they were on their way.

Josh rolled down the passenger window and reached for Taylor's hand. "I'm sorry, sweetheart. There isn't room in the plane."

Shane turned the keys in the ignition and Taylor said, "I'll see you at the hospital…as soon as I get Dad and Michael home."

Jenny started crying in the back seat and Shane threw the gearshift in reverse. The car started to move and Taylor let go of Josh's hand. He stuck his head out the window and shouted something. "I—"

But he was gone and she couldn't hear him.

When she turned around, Ryder was hustling Buck and Billy into the back seat of Max's Lincoln while Savannah buckled the baby in the car seat and then jumped into the front.

Taylor spotted Michael and her dad walking her way. She shot a nervous glance at her father who moved slowly toward her car. He looked older than she'd ever seen him…and something else. Stunned, perhaps. The way he'd looked standing near her mother's grave the day of the funeral.

They reached her and she said, "You probably heard—"

Michael answered. "Who didn't? But can Josh fly like that? I mean—"

"Yes. He has hand controls. He'll do fine." She watched as Dad just stood there. His shoulders were drooped, hands buried deep in his pockets, fingers jingling loose change as he sometimes did when he was troubled. She touched his shoulder, and he jumped. "Dad?"

"Don't worry about me." He bent into the back seat and shut the door. "Nothing a good night's sleep won't cure."

Taylor stared at him a moment, then slid behind the wheel. If he didn't look better by the time they reached Bozeman, she'd take him to the hospital with her instead of dropping him off. She backed down the gravel drive thinking she would feel a lot better if they weren't two hours from their destination.

In the darkness Taylor squinted at the rearview mirror. Her dad's eyes were closed and he appeared to be dozing.

The roads were dry and traffic light, so she took advantage of Montana's no-speed-limit law and made it to Bozeman in record time.

As they neared the city lights, Michael leaned over and whispered, "I'd rather go to the hospital with you than hang around the apartment and miss all the action."

"It could be a long night, Michael."

"Didn't you say it was a short walk to the apartment?"

She weighed the options a moment, then said, "I don't want to leave Dad alone. He doesn't look well."

Michael turned his head and looked in the back.

John straightened in his seat and yawned. "What are you two whispering about up there?"

Taylor caught Michael's eye. He nodded and said, "I was going to go to the hospital with sis, but she's right. You don't look so good, Pop. She's going to drop us both at the apartment."

"All I needed was some rest. I just got it. So let's go."

Michael asked, "You sure?"

"Positive. Got my second wind now."

Taylor wanted to argue but decided the hospital might be best, anyway. Maybe she'd have a doctor check him over, be sure he was all right.

She pulled into the parking lot and they all got out. "Michael...you go ahead. Tell Josh and the others I'll be right there. I want to talk to Dad a minute." Michael shot a concerned look at his father, then did as he was asked.

Taylor turned around and her father was jingling his change again. "Dad...I'm worried about you. As long as we're here, I'd like you to see a doctor."

He slumped against the side of the car, letting out a weary sigh. Then his head came up slowly and his eyes met hers. "Taylor...I'm not sick, but—" he glanced away, then back "—we have to talk."

She pulled him toward her for a hug, assuming she knew the source of the sadness she saw in his eyes. Suddenly he clasped her shoulders and held her at arm's length.

"I—it's about your mother's journals."

Nonplussed, she fell back a step. Of all the things he might have said, she wasn't prepared for this one. She looked away, not wanting him to see how much she knew, but he turned her head back with his finger and stared into her eyes.

"You know, don't you?"

She closed her eyes and bought a few more precious seconds. Her mother had asked her to find the journals. If only she had destroyed them, if she had never read—

"Did you take them from the attic, Taylor?"

She started to open her mouth, but nothing came out. Then she nodded slowly and saw the searing pain in her father's eyes.

He dropped his hands to his sides and fell back against the car again, looking as though the world had come crashing down upon him. "But you haven't told Michael, have you."

It was more a statement than a question. He knew she wouldn't. She looked at the broken man in front of her and wondered what she could say to comfort him? It was obvious he knew what the journals said and that he had kept his discovery from his wife. Yet still, after all these years and no infidelity on Mom's part, why—

Her father raised his chin and his glassy eyes caught a ray of light from a street lamp. He held her steady gaze for a painful moment, then choked out his biggest fear in a sudden rush of words. "Please…I beg of you…don't ever tell Michael that I'm not—" he gulped for air "—that Max is his—" His shoulders started to heave and then came the racking sobs.

Taylor stared at her ravaged father's face, her own shock freezing her in place. Surely he didn't know what he was saying…he couldn't think that Michael…Mom had said she would never break her vows. There was nothing in the journal that had said she had.

Dad clutched her arm, swiping at his wet cheeks with

the back of his free hand. "I should have burned those books when I found them." He wrinkled his face in self-disgust and shook his head from side to side. "Especially the second one. No one else ever had to know..."

The second one.

She pictured it in the nightstand at the farm. Unfinished. When Dad had asked if she knew, she'd assumed he meant Mom's feelings for Max.

Now she knew what the second one would have revealed had she finished it, and her heart splintered into tiny shards.

Shock was soon replaced with panic as the truth worked its way from her stomach to her brain. Michael—her dear, sweet, innocent brother.

No. Her half brother.

She shook her head. The truth wouldn't compute. She pictured his young, handsome face. Then she thought of Max and tried to put them side by side in her mind. It just couldn't be.

"Please, Taylor. Promise me—"

Taylor let out a choked breath and pulled her father to her. He clung to her tightly, waiting for her to say the right words.

If what she'd just learned was indeed true, Michael deserved to know. Yet hearing her father gasping for breath over her shoulder, she felt no choice but to assure him his secret was safe. In a hoarse whisper she said, "I promise, Daddy."

He let out a loud breath but didn't loosen his grip. Finally she pulled back and looked up at his stricken face. And still, her heart refused to believe her ears. She wished they could abandon this subject and never refer to it again, except she had one more question to ask, and she had to ask it now or she knew she never would. "D-did you ever take tests? Maybe—"

He interrupted her. "Like the book said, that case of mumps I had at such a late age...the doctor told us sterility was common...that's why we filed for adoption. We were put on a long list and didn't know if we'd ever have another child.'' He pulled a handkerchief from his rear pocket, wiped his faced again and blew his nose. When he was finished, he straightened his back and began again.

"I couldn't love Michael more if he were my very own blood.''

Taylor took both of her father's hands and squeezed them tight. "I know that, Dad.'' He eyed her tenderly and she fought giving in to her own pain. Later, she thought, when she was alone. Right now Dad needed her love and strength. And she would give it to him. Unconditionally.

"Dad...I'm taking you back to the apartment.'' He started to argue, but she opened the door and nudged him into the front seat. The last thing he needed was to spend the night in a hospital waiting room with Max Malone. She wondered how she would even manage to face Max without him knowing what she'd just learned. For Dad, it would be an impossible task.

As they pulled out of the hospital parking lot, he said in a choked voice. "Michael—''

"Maybe someday you'll tell him, Dad, but he won't hear it from me. I promise.''

"Max and Josh, too? You won't tell anyone?''

She caught a red light and closed her eyes a moment. How could she possibly hope for a future with Josh and keep such a secret from him? His words at the farm after she'd moved back to the ranch echoed in her head: *I know you'd never intentionally keep something important from me...something you knew I'd want or need to know.* She remembered her answer, too: *Yes. You're right. I wouldn't.*

"Taylor?''

She bit her top lip and looked into the eyes of the man who had always been her rock, who had always been there for her, no matter what the circumstance. "No one, Daddy. I promise.''

The light changed and soon they pulled to a stop in front of her apartment. With trembling fingers, she removed the key from the chain and handed it to her father. "Maybe I should go up with you...stay a while."

He shook his head, leaned across the seat and pressed his dry lips to her cheek. Then he turned and opened the door. She watched him pull himself up the front steps and walk inside. She stayed until the lights came on upstairs and then she pulled out onto the narrow deserted street and made her way back to the hospital, not remembering how she got there.

Sobs pushed at her throat again and this time she gave in.

In the waiting room upstairs, Buck took Billy to the rest room and Savannah leaned over to Ryder. "Where are you? You seem a million miles away?"

Ryder looked in the direction of his father, who was standing next to Michael, both watching fireworks somewhere in the distance. The pair were far enough away that Ryder decided to take a chance and tell Savannah what was on his mind. He hunched closer and whispered, "That long talk I had with Dad a couple years ago...about his past...when I asked him some rather pointed questions—"

Savannah stole a glimpse at Max and then rolled her hand at Ryder as if to say hurry up and say it.

"He admitted to having an affair with a nurse in Ann Arbor. I can't help but wonder if—"

Billy sauntered back to them, hopped into the chair next to Ryder, and the conversation stopped.

"What were you guys talking about? Nothing wrong with Aunt Jenny or the babies, is there?"

Ryder patted Billy's knee. "No, buddy. Everything is fine so far. These things usually take a long time."

He rolled his eyes. "I know. I remember when my brother was born. I thought Savannah would never stop crying." He frowned and cocked his head. "Do you think Aunt Jenny is crying?"

Ryder and Savannah exchanged a knowing look, then noticed Josh wheeling toward them.

Josh spotted his father with Michael near the window, but Taylor was nowhere in sight. Maybe she was down in the PT room, checking on a patient. He rolled closer to his brother. "Anyone see Taylor?" Ryder and Savannah shook their heads. Josh turned to Billy. "How about you, sport?"

"Nope."

The baby started crying. Savannah patted his back and rocked him, but it didn't work. She got up and they headed for the hall. Ryder and Billy, looking restless themselves, pushed out of their chairs and followed her, leaving Josh with his thoughts.

He turned one wheel and looked around, hoping to see Taylor's smiling face ambling toward him. A gray-haired volunteer and what looked like grandparents-to-be sat quietly reading, but no Taylor.

He slumped in his chair and heaved a sigh, only to feel worse when he heard the crackling and booming sounds of fireworks outside. His own at home would have to wait for another night.

As would his marriage proposal.

He fingered the small box in his pocket to be sure it was still there. It was. His grandmother's ring. Taylor would love it and he knew she would say yes. Except this wasn't the time or place to ask her. But ask her he would.

As soon as the time was right.

He looked over his shoulder at his father and Michael and decided to ask them about Taylor's whereabouts. Surely one of them would know. As he drew nearer, he heard snippets of their conversation. Michael was talking about carpentry and his apprenticeship training, and Josh wished he'd joined them earlier. Carpentry was one of his favorite subjects and he wanted to get to know Michael better. Their time earlier had been so short.

Apparently they didn't hear Josh coming since neither

turned or acknowledged him. He felt as though he were eavesdropping, but he was waiting for a place to jump in.

Max, with his hands locked behind his back and casually rocking back on his heels, asked Michael another question. "So that would make you about twenty-two or so now?"

"Uh-uh. Started my training early...in high school. I just turned twenty."

Josh noticed his father's change in posture. He stopped rocking and his fingers locked tighter together. Maybe he was wondering how many beers Michael had had at the party since he wasn't of age yet. Dad could be a stickler for such things. Josh cleared his throat, deciding now was a good time to ask his own question and at the same time save Michael the lecture.

Max turned, his eyes dark as coals, and at first Josh didn't think his father recognized who was in front of him.

"Where are you two hiding Taylor?" Josh asked, ignoring his father's strange behavior.

Michael glanced around and seemed surprised Taylor wasn't in the room. "She was talking with Dad in the parking lot when I came up...said she'd be right in." He ran his hand across the back of his neck, his eyebrows pinching together. "Dad looked pretty beat. Maybe she took him back to the apartment."

Josh looked to his dad in hopes of learning more, but he was facing the window again, looking lost in his thoughts. Most likely he was worried about Jenny and the babies. Twins born a month early were at risk. Jenny had surely expressed those concerns often enough on the flight here.

There was a bank of pay phones at the end of the hall. Josh decided to call the apartment and see if anyone was there. Michael was probably right. Taylor took her father home and she would be back any moment, but he wanted to be sure everything was okay.

He touched his pocket again and smiled. He couldn't wait to see the expression on her face when the right time came and he finally popped the question.

Fifteen

Taylor used a phone off the first-floor lobby, called Labor and Delivery upstairs, then returned to her car and drove back home on automatic pilot.

They had stopped Jenny's labor and it could be days or even weeks before anything happened. There was no point going upstairs. Michael had volunteered to walk home or someone would give him a lift. Right now she needed time to calm down, time to think, time to decide how to reconcile her promises to two men who meant the world to her.

The only thing she seemed certain of at the moment was the fact that she couldn't look Josh in the eye without him knowing something was weighing heavily on her mind. And he would demand a truth she couldn't share.

Somehow she had to find a way to work things out. But not tonight. First she would see what she could do to help Dad. Then later she'd think about the problem with Josh and, God willing, find a solution.

When she let herself in, the apartment was dark and quiet. In silhouette she saw her father rocking near the window.

He stopped and asked, "How are the babies and Jenny?"

She told him what little she knew, and he started rocking again. "Michael will probably be along shortly."

The silence stretched until he asked, "Did you see Josh?"

"No. I—I can't right now."

"He'll call, you know. What will you tell him?"

She sat on the floor next to the rocker and rehashed an earlier idea. Josh wouldn't like it. He wouldn't understand. But hopefully soon...*please, God, soon*...she'd find a way to face him.

"I'm going to the ranch to pick up some of my things, and I'll be back by morning. Tell him I'm going to stay here with you and Michael, that I want to take you to Yellowstone Park, Beartooth Highway and whatever else we can squeeze in. Tell him I'll call in a couple of days."

Her father sucked in a long breath and let it out slowly. "I'm so sorry, sweetheart."

She rested her head on the arm of the rocker, and he stroked her hair. "It's not your fault, Dad." She wanted to say it was no one's fault, but that would only hurt him more. How painful it must have been for him to read Mom's words of passion and desire for another man. How sad for them all.

"Is there anything else I can do?" her father asked.

"Tell Josh to leave a message on my machine if there's any news about the babies. I'll check often from wherever we are."

She pushed off the floor and started to leave, then rushed back and flung her arms around her father's neck, wishing she were a little girl again, that she could climb up on his lap, that she was still naive about the realities of the adult world. "I love you, Daddy." She started to cry, in spite of all efforts not to.

He held her tight, and she could feel his own tears wet her hair. "I love you, too, Taylor." He made a hiccuping sound, then added, "And Michael...with all my heart."

"I know. I know." She kissed his forehead and went out the door before she could change her mind. It would be a long night, driving to Joeville and back. But for now she saw no other way.

Josh hung up the phone and stared into the darkness beyond the window. This was meant to be one of the happiest nights of his life, and everything was falling apart around him. Ryder and his family, along with Michael, had passed him and waved goodbye while he was talking on the phone to Taylor's dad, with Ryder looking especially eager to leave. Dad was still at the window with his head down. Buck sat trancelike in the waiting room, and now John Phillips provided the last puzzling blow—Taylor wasn't home and wouldn't be for some time. They were going sightseeing for a couple of days, he had said. She'd be in touch.

What in the hell was going on? Was he the only one in the dark? He knew the family was worried about the babies, but his gut told him there was something more. Especially with Taylor. In the past he would have been outraged by her behavior, but it was obvious something ominous had invaded their world, sending everything spinning out of orbit, leaving more than himself feeling adrift.

And it was time that he got to the bottom of it.

He pushed the wheels hard and closed the distance to his father, calling out his name before he stopped. "Dad?"

Max looked over his shoulder, and Josh knew he had been right. But first they would find a place alone and they would talk.

"Dad...I'm feeling sort of antsy and stiff. Mind going to the PT room and working with me for a while?"

Max stared at him as he had before.

"I know it's late, but—"

"Yes, yes." He shook his head as if to clear it. "Sure, son. Let's do that." He grabbed the handles of the chair, and they passed Buck, who didn't blink or speak.

The PT room was locked, but Max found the key and flicked the light switch on. He moved straight for the bars and adjusted them to the correct height and then busied himself with selecting various weights until Josh ran out of patience.

"Dad...stop." Max turned slowly. "You have to tell me." Max started to speak too quickly and Josh cut him off. "The truth, Dad. The big secret that seems to be on everyone's mind but mine." He didn't like his accusatory tone, so he changed it. "Ryder knows something. Buck and Mary know. Now Taylor, her father...and you. Whatever it is, it's affecting me, too. Taylor's leaving town for a while and didn't even say goodbye. That's not like her, Dad."

Josh kept his gaze fixed on his father's, who acted as though he were struggling with something beyond his control, a bewildered man who was clearly deciding how much to say and the right way to say it. Finally he pulled a weight bench closer to Josh and straddled the end. He placed his elbows on his knees, let out a weary sigh and told Josh everything he knew for certain and even the parts he had speculated on as this traumatic night had unfolded.

When Max had finished, Josh stared at him open-mouthed. "Th-then Michael could be—"

Max nodded, his eyes begging for forgiveness.

The possibility and all its ramifications throbbed at Josh's temples, and he massaged his pulse points. He could feel his father's pain. He could only imagine John's. Assuming John knew. He remembered seeing the change in John's demeanor after his father had arrived at the party. John and Taylor had stayed in the hospital parking lot and talked. Neither had come up.

Yes. John knew.

And Taylor.

What must this be doing to her? She couldn't have known before tonight or he would have noticed something. Then what happened? There were so many questions and so few answers.

Yet somewhere in this mess he felt hope. These were all good people. Together they had to find an answer.

"Dad...did you get any indication that Michael might know...or even suspect?" Josh asked, already guessing the answer.

Max shook his head slowly from side to side.

"This has to be the reason Taylor took off without talking to me." Josh said, as much to himself as to his father, still groping for solutions. An idea rose to the surface, and he decided to give it voice. "What if I found Taylor and told her we know about Michael?...assure her we would never discuss it with him or anyone else?"

Max thought a moment, then looked even more grim. "You were planning a future with Taylor, and now—"

Josh remembered the ring box and pulled it out of his pocket, refusing to believe all was lost. "By the way, thanks for enlisting Hannah's help. Look." He opened the black velvet box and lifted it for his father to see. "It was your mother's. Grandma gave it to Hannah for safekeeping...said Hannah would know who to give it to when the time came." He looked at the ring wistfully. "I was going to give it to Taylor during the fireworks."

Max closed his eyes and tilted his head back. It took him a while to speak and Josh waited patiently, praying for a miracle.

Finally Max's gaze locked on Josh's, and a small smile creased his father's haggard face. "If I could have picked from all the women in the world, I couldn't have done better for you than Taylor. She already feels like part of the family." He sobered quickly, the lines in his forehead pronounced. "But would she ever want me as her father-in-law? Would she want to see me day after day and remember what I did to her family?" He stood and started pacing the length of the room, while Josh weighed his father's questions.

From all that Josh had seen, Taylor had almost hero-worshipped his father. Could she find it in her heart to forgive him? And would this sin tarnish the memory of her mother whom she loved so much?

His earlier optimism was starting to wane as he thought of the magnitude of their problems.

His father strode back to the bench and sat down. "I know what I did was inexcusable, but you deserve to know more." He drifted off to some dark corner of his past and spoke in a faraway voice. "Right after your mom…died, I found out certain things…things that made me so angry I couldn't see straight. That's when I returned to Ann Arbor for a while…to get away."

Josh knew what his father was referring to. They had all learned years ago about his mother's infidelity. But Josh let his father vent without comment.

"Angela and I had been friends when I worked there twice before. I'd felt something special between us, but I'd managed to keep things on the up and up. She was married and had a daughter. And I had never cheated on your mother." He shook his head, and Josh could see his father reliving that painful period of his life.

"I lost a friend—a colleague—in surgery one night…. Angela was assisting. She came to my office later to comfort me. It started with just a gentle touch to my cheek." His red-rimmed eyes met Josh's. "It only happened that once. I came back here soon after. Josh…I never knew about—"

Josh stared at the ceiling and breathed deeply, his chest feeling his father's heartbreak and guilt.

"Can you ever forgive me, son?"

Josh wheeled his chair closer and clutched his dad's arm. "There's nothing to forgive, Dad." He purposely held his father's stricken gaze, refusing to be the first to look away.

Max stood abruptly and looked down at his son, a determined set to his jaw. He exhaled loudly. "Joshua...I caused this problem...and I'm going to fix it."

Josh waited for an explanation, wondering if anything could fix it.

"I'm going to see John. Now."

John insisted Michael use Taylor's bedroom, explaining she wouldn't be home until morning and that he wasn't ready for bed. Michael found his headphones, went to Taylor's room, closed the door and was sound asleep by the time John heard Max's slow, heavy steps making their way up to the second floor.

John opened the door and the two men took each other's measure. Before tonight, neither had expected to face the other. But that was before John's daughter and Max's son had fallen in love. Both would endure anything for their children.

John headed for the kitchen, turned on a light and sat at the small table. Max sat across from him. Their words were spoken softly. Terse and to the point. Their objectives were simple: to discuss Michael and to find a way to help Josh and Taylor through this muddy maze.

When Max asked about Michael's blood type, John couldn't recall. But he did remember the soiled towel in the sink. Max bagged the towel and John was right on his heels as they left for the hospital.

Within minutes Max was rousting an emergency technician from her sleep. The bag was handed over, and then blood and saliva were extracted from both men. Testing was conducted by the yawning woman while two fathers leaned against the wall outside. Finally Max turned to John.

"I told her to find me, if we weren't here when she was done. My office would be more comfortable...discreet."

They walked down the hall side by side in stony silence. Once inside Max's office, with the door shut behind them, Max went to the window and spoke over his shoulder.

"Sterility from mumps isn't always permanent, you know."

John slumped into a chair on the other side of the desk. "It never really mattered to me. I loved my wife…and Michael was mine from the day he was born." He paused, then more to himself than to Max, he said, "Guess I wanted to pretend there was a chance…I was afraid a test would…"

He didn't finish. He didn't have to.

There seemed nothing else to say, so they waited—one man hoping for a miracle and the other feeling selfish for entertaining thoughts of a different outcome, one that might connect him forever to Angela and provide living evidence of a love that never had a chance.

But in his heart Max knew the outcome that would make life easier for everyone else, so to that end he prayed and waited and remembered.

At the ranch Taylor tiptoed up the back steps in the kitchen and filled her suitcase with the essentials; the rest she could get another time. Then she went to the farm and retrieved the journals she'd left in the nightstand drawer. Her plan had been to get in and out as quickly as possible and back to Bozeman. Yet now, looking around the rooms that had held gaiety and laughter just hours before, she slumped on a large floor pillow in front of the cold hearth and clutched the books to her chest.

The room was dark and chilly. She shivered as much from the events of the day as from the cool summer night. She hugged herself tight and looked around. This was the house she had hoped would become her home someday. The home she and Josh would fill with love, laughter and the playful sounds of happy little ones.

Silent tears streamed down her face. How could that ever happen now? She couldn't keep this or any secret from Josh, and even if she could, wouldn't her father feel betrayed on some level? Especially living and working so closely with Max now that she knew the truth?

She stood and walked to the nearest lamp and turned it on. Then she found newspaper and made paper knots—the way Josh had taught her. She stacked a few logs in the grate, stuffed the knots in strategic places and struck a match to the pile. And when the flames licked over the logs she set the journals in her lap and eyed them.

She could read the rest of book two, but what would that tell her? That Mom and Max had given in to their feelings for each other? She already knew that. And on the long drive here, she'd also figured out the timing of things. Max's wife committed suicide about a year before Michael's birth. She remembered hearing Max had returned to Ann Arbor for a short third stint. Her mother was a warm and compassionate person. Maybe it just happened once; maybe not. A part of her wanted to know the whole story. A bigger part—her conscience—told her it was none of her business.

Slowly she began tearing the pages from their bindings and fed them to the flames, watching as her mother's words of love, anguish and imperfection were blackened, curled and reduced to ashes.

Taylor tore at the pages faster and faster, feeling a mix of anger and pity, love and frustration, until at last they were all gone and she tossed the calico covers on top of it all.

With one last, lingering look, Taylor walked outside and found Hank stretching and yawning outside the bunkhouse. She rushed over, filled him in on Jenny's status, and then asked him to keep an eye on the fire until it went out. As usual he agreed without question.

On the highway back to Bozeman, the adrenaline began to ebb, and she stopped at a convenience store for a large cup of coffee and then spent the rest of the drive planning some sight-seeing for the next few days. One way or the other, she would put everything else on hold and enjoy the brief time she had with her dad and Michael. After they left, maybe she would be able to face Josh without him seeing the dark secret in her eyes or the broken pieces of her heart.

Before dawn Max found Josh in the waiting room and told him everything that had been discussed with John. Even the results of the tests.

Josh rested his elbows on his knees and hung his head between his arms, tired beyond sleep and emotionally spent. It was impossible to gauge how this new information would impact his relationship with Taylor. The damage had been done. So many people had been staggered by this night that he wondered if anything would ever be the same again.

Max sat down next to him. "You need rest, Josh. There's nothing more you can do now. John said he'd talk with Taylor before he left town. Let the family have a few days of vacation, then when John and Michael go home…well, you'll see.

"Let her come to you, Josh…when she's ready. She needs time to adjust to all this. But I know Taylor, and so do you. She'll come around. In the meantime, I got us some beds here at the hospital. This way we can keep tabs on Jenny and the babies…and we can work our butts off getting you out of that chair for good."

At last Josh smiled and met his father's eyes. "Sounds like a plan to me, Dad." Max turned Josh's chair around and wheeled him out of the room and Josh added, "Thanks, Dad…for everything."

Max gave a self-deprecating chuckle. "Well…not for everything."

Sixteen

Taylor had barely gotten home and asleep when she smelled coffee brewing in the kitchen. Dad and Michael were pulling things from the refrigerator and cupboards as quietly as they could, but the apartment was small, and she couldn't help but hear the slightest sound.

She rolled over and with one eye read the green numbers on her alarm clock: 9:30. She struggled to a sitting position, her limbs sluggish with exhaustion, her mind still on overload from the events of the past twenty-four hours.

Sunshine streamed through the miniblinds, and she squinted at the view beyond them. The weatherman promised a gorgeous day, and her family would be eager to see the sights. At least Michael would. She wondered how her father was doing this morning. He and Michael had been sound asleep on the sofa bed when she'd finally arrived home.

She pushed off the bed, shrugged into her favorite chenille robe and then said a sleepy 'morning as she made a quick dash to the only bathroom. A little more time and a cold shower—that's what she needed before putting on her tour guide face. And coffee. Lots of it. The spray hit her face and she started to come around, determined to make the best of the next few days.

She dressed quickly and joined the men in the kitchen. Dad looked up from his eggs and smiled at her. A tired smile, but nonetheless a smile, which she took as a good sign that things were on the mend.

Michael handed her some eggs and refilled her coffee. "Sorry I left your bed a mess. Dad dragged me out in the middle of the night."

Taylor chuckled. "Not to worry. I don't even remember hitting the mattress." She drank more coffee and then started running through the day's plan. "I was thinking we'd go down to Yellowstone, spend some time there, then take Beartooth Highway to the east and then north to Red Lodge. I made a reservation there for the night, but we could keep going if you're in the mood."

"I looked on the map earlier," Michael said. "That's quite a hike without any stops—maybe a couple hundred miles."

Dad set his cup down. "I vote for Red Lodge and taking our time. I even bought one of those throwaway cameras in case we see any animals."

Taylor laughed, feeling the effects of the caffeine and beginning to believe they could have a good time in spite of yesterday. "Oh, I think you might see an animal or two. And you'll want a picture of me and Michael having a snowball fight. Beartooth's at about eleven thousand feet— animals, mountains, wildflowers and snow." She picked up dishes and walked to the sink, eager to hit the road. "You'll never want to go home."

Shortly after ten, they piled into Taylor's Ford and headed east for Livingston before picking up 540 and turning south for Yellowstone National Park. For the first few miles she thought about the Malones and the mess she was leaving behind. When it started to hurt too much, she forced herself to put it away for later. She needed this time away from them—especially Max and Josh—to put things into perspective. Besides, Michael and Dad would be gone all too soon. Michael might return someday, but somehow she doubted her father ever would. The thought made her feel sad, but she mentally shook herself, more determined than ever to enjoy their brief visit.

She had planned this time in her head for so many years; she couldn't allow anything to ruin it now.

Early Saturday evening, one week after the Fourth, Shane entered the Physical Therapy Unit with that special smile reserved for new papas. He closed the door and strutted across the room. In spite of hospital rules, he handed his father and Josh each a cigar and the three of them lit up together.

Josh was sitting in a chair along the wall. He leaned forward and said, "Well? Are we going to have to guess or are you going to tell us?"

Shane emitted another cloud of smoke and milked the moment. "Two absolutely gorgeous little girls. Both mama and babies doing fine. They're a little small, but perfectly okay."

Max gripped Shane's hand and slapped his back. "Girls. Finally!" He shook his head. "They're going to be spoiled rotten, you know."

Shane sat down and crossed a leg over a knee. "That's the plan."

Joshua watched his brother's face and shared his joy, yet he had to admit that he was envious, too.

It had been a week since he'd seen Taylor, and he wondered now if she would ever call. He knew Michael and John must have left days ago to go back to Ann Arbor and still no word from Taylor. So far he had listened to his dad's advice and waited for her to come to him when she was ready. But now he didn't think he could wait much longer, certainly not indefinitely. If he didn't hear from her before the weekend was over, then he would call her.

Shane stopped puffing and said to his dad, "Hope you don't mind that Jenny wanted you to wait down here. She was a little self-conscious having her father-in-law around."

"I totally understand. I just would have been in the way, anyway."

Shane laughed. "Though before it was over, I don't think modesty was on her mind anymore." He shook his head. "I'm sure glad I'm a man."

They all laughed and agreed. Then Shane asked, "Where's Taylor? She's missing all the excitement."

Josh and Max exchanged a quick glance and Max said, "She took some time off to be with her family... sightseeing."

Shane frowned. "But didn't they leave—"

Josh rubbed out his cigar in the ashtray that Max passed him and changed the subject. "Think you can handle some more good news today?"

"You'll have a hard time topping the twins, but go for it."

Max handed Josh a pair of crutches and Josh hoisted himself up, enjoying the look on Shane's face. With practiced skill, Josh crossed the room unassisted, his legs doing all the work, the crutches clearly there for security only. Then he turned and came back to his brother. "What do you think about that?"

Shane stood and stared openmouthed, taking his time looking at Josh from head to toe and back up. He started to speak, then thrust his arms around Josh and thumped his back. "Thank God, thank God." He stepped back, his eyes misted over.

"You're not going to go cry on me, are you big brother?"

Shane widened his eyes, blinked and chuckled. "Hell, no. Real cowboys don't cry."

"Uh-huh." Josh sat down and grinned up at him. "You don't happen to have a video of the twins' births, do you?"

Shane pulled a handkerchief from his hip pocket and blew his nose. "Well, that's different."

They were still laughing when the phone on the corner desk started ringing. Max crossed over and answered it. Whoever was on the other end was asking about the newborns and Max was happily relaying details. When he was done, he turned and smiled at Josh.

"It's for you."

Josh looked at his father's face and instantly knew. He grabbed the crutches beside him and made it to the desk in record time. Breathless, he took the receiver and watched his father walk away, taking Shane with him.

"Hello?" There was no response for the longest time, but he could hear breathing.

"Hi," she finally said, and his heart soared.

"Taylor...I've missed—"

"I'm sorry I took so—"

"I've got so much to—"

"We need to talk," she said, laughing. "In person. I don't think this way is working too well."

He loved her laugh, the sound of her voice, everything about her. Finally he remembered what he'd planned to say if she ever called. "Can you meet me at the airport? Go for a ride?"

"Now?"

"That's not soon enough."

"Meet you there in half an hour." She hung up and he replaced the receiver.

He sat down, caught his breath and then made the necessary calls.

Josh hid his crutches under the back seat, patted the pocket of his aviator jacket and tried not to hyperventilate when he saw Taylor crossing the tarmac. Her hair was whipping across her face and he thought she'd never looked more beautiful.

She climbed into the seat next to him, as if she had every day, and flashed him a big smile. "Hi, cowboy."

He met and held her gaze, seeing she was as nervous as he was. There was so much that needed to be said. But not yet. They weren't going to shout their words over the engine. What they needed to say, must be said softly, with nothing to distract them. He smiled at her before he looked ahead and taxied down the runway.

The sun had just set when they neared the first cluster of mountains, the reddish look of alpenglow fading to shades of rose and lavender as they flew over in silence. Families of deer ate at clearings here and there, and the plane's dark shadow reflected in still waters below.

Neither said a word, but simply enjoyed the majesty of it all.

Josh checked the GPS and knew they were getting close. He dropped to a lower elevation, barely clearing the dense forest of evergreens that separated them from the tower a few miles ahead. He glanced over and saw the serene smile on Taylor's face and he had no doubt she knew where they were going.

He circled once and checked that the grassy field alongside was clear of animals and then he set her down gently, rolling to a stop a short distance from the ladder.

Taylor opened the door and dropped the steps, giving Josh one last smile before she left the plane. He fumbled nervously for his crutches and then sidestepped to the door, trying not to be intimidated by the stairs. When he was on the ground in front of her, she grinned and walked beside him to the tower's tall wooden ladder. He dropped one crutch at a time and gripped the sides of the ladder. Then, with a couple of deep breaths, he began the long climb, taking one step at a time and not looking up or down. His arms trembled and he stopped to rest. He could hear Taylor behind him and suddenly he worried about falling on her.

He gritted his teeth and began again, his breathing coming in short gulps, beads of sweat running into his eyes. And then he saw the railing of the observation deck and he was there.

He turned and sat down on the white painted platform that surrounded the glass enclosure behind him, his chest rising and falling, heart pounding. And facing him was the happiest, sweetest face he had ever seen. He started to laugh, as much from nerves as the foolhardy stunt he'd just pulled, and Taylor laughed, too, their voices carrying across the treetops and floating off into the still night. Finally he held out a hand and she came up the rest of the way and sat beside him. He turned and looked at her.

"Well? You don't seem the least bit surprised. Aren't you going to say something?"

"I love you, Joshua Malone."

"No, I mean about—" He stopped and stared at her, not believing what he just heard. "Just like that?" he asked when he'd recovered.

"Just like that."

He wanted to say "I love you, too" and pull the ring from his pocket this very second. But with great control, he held back. It could wait a little longer. Besides, he didn't want the word *too* in there the first time. And there were matters to clear up, the sooner the better.

"Mind sitting here awhile…and talking?"

She looked out over the trees and exhaled a long breath. "I assume Max told you about Michael."

"Yes, he did. And he told me about the tests, too."

She looked straight ahead. "I didn't even know they had gone to the hospital that night. Dad was asleep when I got home from the farm. The next morning we started our trip and he acted as if nothing had happened." Josh took her hand and she continued. "He left a letter under my pillow that I found when they were gone. He said he didn't want to ruin our vacation."

"Did you say anything about…well—"

She looked at him. "That the tests proved Max is definitely Michael's father?" She nodded her head. "Yes. But he said he always knew, that it didn't change anything. He also asked that we not let this come between us. He knows how I feel about you and he's happy for us." She smiled. "He said he even liked you."

Josh held her gaze, afraid to ask the next question. "But will it be a problem? For you and Dad? For us?"

She shook her head slowly and he felt the air rush out of his lungs.

"Someday I'll tell you about Mom's journals that I read, but not tonight. Let me just say…it wasn't all your father's fault, Josh." She looked pensive for a moment, then said, "Behind Dad and Michael, Max has been the third most important man in my life for years." She smiled. "He's only slipped to number four."

It was dark now but clear, and millions of stars burned bright in the big sky all around them. Josh held her hand and didn't care if they ever moved.

"There's one more thing," she said after a while. "Dad said he planned to tell Michael the truth someday soon. He just wanted a little time to figure out the best way to say it." She paused, and he thought she was finished. Then she added. "I know Michael. He'll be more worried about how Dad feels than himself. It will all work out okay." Then, as if to herself, she said, "I wouldn't be surprised if he came back here sometime…and talked with Max. Eventually he'll want to know everything."

"And how do you feel about that?" Josh asked.

She nodded slowly. "Okay. I love all three of them, and I know they won't mess things up. It'll be okay."

Josh expelled a long breath and wrapped his arm around her. "Ready to go inside?"

She snuggled closer and shivered from the cool night's breeze. "How 'bout if I open the door, grab you under the arms and just drag you in?" She chuckled softly into his chest.

"How 'bout if you go inside and get the other pair of crutches Ryder dropped off?"

She pulled back and smiled. "You've thought of everything, haven't you?"

He thought of the ring in his pocket. "Yep."

Taylor got the crutches and helped him up, and they entered the rustic quarters with its windowed walls on all sides. Josh watched her pivot in the middle of the room, her eyes catching slivers of starlight as she turned.

"It's just as awesome as you said."

Josh lit a propane lamp and settled onto a cracked leather sofa in front of one view and patted the seat beside him. She sat close and snuggled beneath his arm.

They fell silent and took it all in. So much had happened, yet here they were. Together. No more secrets. No more games.

After a while Josh said, "I think we should come back here every year on this day." He chuckled. "It may be the only penthouse I'll be able to afford for a while."

"Yeah, right." She poked him in the ribs and he jumped.

"Really. We better have a good crop next year or I'm broke."

She laughed out loud. "Joshua Malone, you don't know what broke is."

"I'm serious." He tried to look serious, but he knew he was grinning.

"Even if that were true, I was never after your money, anyway."

He smiled, seeing the opening she had just given him. "I know you weren't. You were never after anything." He kissed the top of her nose and kept his face close. "That's why I love you. That's why I think I loved you that day you flew back to Detroit, maybe even before that."

In the dim light he could see her eyes turn glassy. He felt around in his pocket and retrieved the small box, pressing it in her hands at long last. She opened it shyly and then gasped, holding it closer to the light.

"It was my grandmother's—Dad's mom. We can always have the stone reset." She hadn't said a word. He wondered if she didn't like it or if something else was wrong. She looked troubled suddenly.

Still eyeing the ring, she said, "It's beautiful, Josh. I love it."

He sighed, only partially relieved. "Taylor? What's wrong?"

She shook her head fast from side to side. "I'm sorry. I-it's just so unexpected." She looked up at him. "I've been checking your charts at the hospital so I wasn't surprised that you could walk. And when you asked me to meet you at the airport, I was sure we'd come here." She looked at the ring. "But this—"

He cupped her chin with his hand, still puzzled by the worry lines on her forehead. "I want to marry you, Taylor...to spend the rest of my life with you at that old farm...and fill it with as many kids as you want." She looked down and he wondered if he'd hit a sensitive note. "You do want kids, don't you?"

A single tear trailed down her cheek as she met his gaze. "Yes, I do. Very much. I see Billy and little Chris...and now the twins...and—"

"And what, sweetheart?" Maybe she couldn't have children and she was afraid to tell him. "If something's wrong, we can always adopt."

She straightened and wiped her cheek. "It's not that, Josh." She heaved a big sigh. "I want to be the one to raise them...like Savannah and Jenny. I don't want someone else to watch our babies' first smiles, when they sit up, when they roll over." She slowed down and took a breath. "I want to marry you, too, Josh. But until my student loans are paid off—" He clasped both her hands in his and tried to speak, but she pushed on. "And no, you aren't going to pay my debts. Besides, you said you were almost broke."

He held a hand over her mouth to silence her and her eyes widened. "Will you let me get a word in edgewise?

Please?'' She nodded and he removed his hand, chuckling and shaking his head. ''This is going to be one hell of a ride—you and me—you know that?''

At last she smiled and rested her head on his shoulder. When she'd calmed down, he pulled an envelope from his pocket and handed it to her.

''What's this?''

''Did I say the surprises were over?''

She looked at her name on the outside. ''It looks like Max's writing.''

''Open it.''

''Have you seen this already?'' He nodded his head and she removed the pages, reading each line slowly.

Dearest Taylor,
I can't begin to express how grateful I am to you for all your hours of dedication and caring—at the hospital, the clinic and especially with my son. Seeing Josh on his feet again is the greatest gift *you* could have given me. And I say *you* because I'm not sure anyone else would have persevered as you did.

For these reasons, and oh, so many more, I wanted to give you something. I asked Josh to pick the time and place to present this letter to you. I pray that you will not misconstrue my motives or be angry with me for what I have done. But this was something I've wanted to do for a very long time.

Please believe me that I did not do this out of guilt or hopes for forgiveness. Though I have plenty of cause for both, I know these things cannot be bought.

Therefore, I hope you enjoy the enclosed and that you trust the spirit in which it is given.

All my best wishes for a bright and happy future.
Fondly, Max

She turned to the next page and there was a copy of her student loan papers...marked Paid in full. She gasped at the last page and eyed Joshua.

"It was all his idea. And you know Dad. When he decides to do something, there's no talking him out of it."

She started to laugh and cry all at the same time. "Who says I want to talk him out of it?" She sprang from the sofa and paced to the glass, then rushed back to him. "Oh, Josh. Do you know what this means?"

He laughed along with her, his nerve endings crackling with her contagious excitement. "That we should start practicing for parenthood right now?" Seeing her this way, he didn't know how much longer he could wait.

"Oh, you." She straddled his lap and started kissing his neck and cheeks and ears, saying "I love you" between each playful peck. Then she stopped and pulled back. "Wait a minute. I don't remember you asking me *the* question."

It took a moment for the blood to travel back to his brain, but then he knew what she wanted. "Taylor Phillips, will you marry me?"

Still laughing and breathless, she held his face firmly in both of her hands and said, "You bet your boots, cowboy. I thought you'd never ask."

*   *   *   *   *

COMING NEXT MONTH

THAT MARRIAGEABLE MAN! Barbara Boswell

Man of the Month

Bachelor Rafe Paradise had his life turned upside down when he 'inherited' four kids. He was determined to be an exceptional *single* father. Then he met his neighbour Holly Casale. Things were changing—fast!—but marriage was still the last thing on his mind—wasn't it?

UNFORGETTABLE BRIDE Annette Broadrick

After a brief wedding of convenience, Casey Carmichael never expected to see Bobby Metcalf again—until she had a phone call. Bobby had lost his memory but he did remember *her*. And he thought they were living as man and wife.

CINDERELLA TWIN Barbara McMahon

Identical Twins

Gorgeous, rich men like Cade Marshall were just a fantasy to librarian Julianne Bennet. Then she secretly swapped lives with her glamorous twin sister and attracted Cade's attention. But how would he react to her deception?

THE BOSS, THE BEAUTY AND THE BARGAIN
Judith McWilliams

When Livvy Farrell asked her boss to masquerade as her fiancé, Conal Sutherland needed *no* persuasion. He'd long been envisioning schemes that moved Livvy from her desk and into his bed. Now he could put them into practice...

MATERNITY BRIDE Maureen Child

The test was positive—Denise Torrance was pregnant after an unexpected night with the man of her dreams! When Mike Ryan insisted that they marry, the passion continued to burn between them...but had she really won his heart?

THE UNLIKELY BODYGUARD Amy J. Fetzer

Calli Thornton was a woman with a mission...to discover fun, adventure—and love! But she was thwarted at every turn by a sexy stranger. Was he trying to stop her having fun, or did he have a completely different agenda?

COMING NEXT MONTH FROM

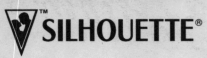 SILHOUETTE®

Sensation
A thrilling mix of passion, adventure and drama

COWBOY COMES HOME Rachel Lee
ROMAN'S HEART Sharon Sala
BLACKWOOD'S WOMAN Beverly Barton
THE VIRGIN AND THE OUTLAW Eileen Wilks

Intrigue
Danger, deception and desire

NOWHERE MAN Rebecca York
NIGHT MIST Helen R .Myers
NICK'S CHILD Tina Vasilos
HEAT OF PASSION Alice Orr

Special Edition
Compelling romances packed with emotion

LITTLE DARLING Cheryl Reavis
SNOWBOUND BRIDE Cathy Gillen Thacker
THE MARRIAGE BARGAIN Jennifer Mikels
THE WEDDING RING PROMISE Susan Mallery
WHO WILL SHE WED? Andrea Edwards
BABY OF MINE Jane Toombs

JOANN
ROSS

a woman's heart

In *A Woman's Heart*, JoAnn Ross has created a
rich, lyrical love story about land, community,
family and the very special bond between a man
who doesn't believe in anything and a woman
who believes in him.

MIRA®　　　**Available from February**

FREE!

4 Books
and a surprise gift!

We would like to take this opportunity to thank you for reading this Silhouette® book by offering you the chance to take FOUR more specially selected titles from the Desire™ series absolutely FREE! We're also making this offer to introduce you to the benefits of the Reader Service™—

- ★ FREE home delivery
- ★ FREE gifts and competitions
- ★ FREE monthly Newsletter
- ★ Books available before they're in the shops
- ★ Exclusive Reader Service discounts

Accepting these FREE books and gift places you under no obligation to buy; you may cancel at any time, even after receiving your free shipment. Simply complete your details below and return the entire page to the address below. *You don't even need a stamp!*

YES! Please send me 4 free Desire books and a surprise gift. I understand that unless you hear from me, I will receive 6 superb new titles every month for just £2.70 each, postage and packing free. I am under no obligation to purchase any books and may cancel my subscription at any time. The free books and gift will be mine to keep in any case.

D9EB

Ms/Mrs/Miss/Mr ....Initials ....
BLOCK CAPITALS PLEASE

Surname ....

Address...

....

....Postcode ....

Send this whole page to:
THE READER SERVICE, FREEPOST CN81, CROYDON, CR9 3WZ
(Eire readers please send coupon to: P.O. Box 4546, DUBLIN 24.)

DIANA PALMER

ONCE in PARIS

Brianne Martin rescued grief-stricken Pierce
Hutton from the depths of despair, but before
she knew it, Brianne had become a pawn in an
international web of deceit and corruption.
Now it was Pierce's turn to rescue Brianne.
What had they stumbled into?
They would be lucky to escape with their lives!

1-55166-470-4
MIRA® Available in paperback from March, 1999

France for £1 with SeaFrance

Here's a really special day out we have arranged with SeaFrance. All our readers can go to France for the day for just £1! And if you want to take your car, until the end of June it's just £20* - and that includes 2 passengers!

To take advantage of this fantastic offer, simply keep the special token overleaf, and look out for the tokens in next month's Silhouette series books. Two different Tokens (from different month's books) can be used to buy your ticket.

How to book:

Once you have collected sufficient tokens, **call the SeaFrance information line** on 0990 711711 and make a booking, telling the operator that you are using Silhouette tokens. See over for Crossing Times.

You can pay either by credit or debit card over the phone, or send a cheque. Either way you will need to **confirm your booking** and send your tokens in, using the Booking Form overleaf, before tickets will be sent to you. You will be given a **Booking Reference Number** when you call. You will need to enter this reference number on the Booking Form. Send completed booking form to: SeaFrance, Eastern Docks, Dover, Kent CT16 1JA. Please allow at least 7 days for delivery of tickets. If you are booking less than 7 days before departure, you must bring the completed Booking Form and tokens (two tokens per person/car) with you when you pick the tickets up from the SeaFrance desk in the Dover Travel Centre in the port, on the day of departure. Car crossings will need to be confirmed using a credit or debit card at the time of telephoning.

Per Foot Passenger	2 different tokens + £1
Per Car (+ 2 Passengers)	Until end June = 2 different tokens + £20
	July - December = 2 different tokens + £50
	Additional car passengers at normal foot passenger rate or 2 tokens + £1.
	NB £10 Saturday Supplement Applies

Exclusions: This offer is not available for travel over bank holiday weekends.

Tokens will be found in all March Silhouette series books, and the vouchers are valid until 31st December 1999.

BOOKING FORM - DAY TRIP TO FRANCE

Send to: SeaFrance, Eastern Docks, Dover, Kent CT16 1JA

Booking Reference Number _____

Name _____

Address _____

_____ PostCode _____

Daytime Tel No. _____ Chosen Date of Travel _____

Chosen Time of Travel _____

I enclose: 2 tokens per person/vehicle = _____ tokens

Cheque made payable to SeaFrance for £ _____ (if applicable)

FEBRUAR

SILHOUET
TOKEN

SEAFRAN
DOVER-CALAIS FER

- -

Terms & Conditions 1. In making this offer, Harlequin Mills & Boon accept no liability for the carriers SeaFrance. 2. There
no limit to the number of tickets you can buy, using this offer, so long as you supply 2 different tokens for each ticket. 3.
Only genuine Silhouette Tokens are valid for this offer. Photocopies will not be accepted. 4. Readers must be 16 or over
participate in this promotion. 5. Tickets are non-transferable and travel must take place on the date booked. 6. The same
number of people must travel on both journeys. 7. You must be in possession of a valid ten year passport. Non EC passp
holders must check EC requirements. 8. Restaurant and shop opening times vary on the Continent and no responsibility
accepted by SeaFrance or the promoters if facilities are closed on the day you travel. 9. This offer is subject to availabili
of space within a special Silhouette readers' allocation. 10. Failure to adhere to the sailing time allocated may lea
to the payment of a supplement. 11. Day trip offers only apply to cars and exclude transit vans, mini buses, camp
vans, trailers and caravans or vehicles carrying freight. 12. SeaFrance's standard booking terms and conditions of
carriage apply to all bookings, together with the special instructions for this offer. Copies available on request.

DAILY CROSSING TIMES

Dover-Calais 00:30; 02:45; 05:15; 08:15; 09:30; 10:45; 12:15; 13:30; 14:45; 16:15; 17:30;
18:45; 20:15; 21:30; 22:45

Calais-Dover 01:45; 04:15; 07:00; 08:20; 09:45; 11:15; 12:30; 13:45; 15:15; 16:30; 17:45;
19:15; 20:30; 21:45; 23:30